Messily Married

Abhishek @B

Leadstart
INKSTATE

ISBN 978-93-5458-836-5

First published in India 2021 by Leadstart Inkstate
A brand of One Point Six Technologies Pvt. Ltd.

123, Building J2, Shram Seva Premises,
Wadala Truck Terminal,
Mumbai 400022, Maharashtra, INDIA
Phone: +91 96999 33000
Email: info@leadstartcorp.com
www.leadstartcorp.com

Disclaimer: This is a work of fiction. All the names, characters, businesses, places, events and incidents in this book are either the product of the author's imagination or used in a fictitious manner. Any resemblance to actual persons, living or dead, or actual events is purely coincidental.

Editor: Sanjhee Gianchandani
Cover: R. Maharaja
Layouts: Kevis Tech

Contents

Acknowledgements

At the very onset, I would like to thank you from the core of my heart, for picking up this book.

With the advent of digitisation, reading itself is becoming an extinct hobby. In such an era, for you to pick up a book to read is extremely commendable.

And then a huge thank you to my friends and colleagues who have always encouraged me to keep on writing after the publication of my first novel, *Lollypops to Cigarettes*.

My deepest gratitude to my young son (Abhinav) and younger spouse (Shrabani), who pushed me to steal time away from my packed schedule to publish my second book.

Last but not the least, I would like to acknowledge the contribution of my publisher, Leadstart Publishing Private Limited, for giving me the platform to concretise my ideas into a tangible form and for helping my book see the light of the day.

Thank you!

ABOUT THE AUTHOR

 Abhishek @B is the short form of the author's full name – **Abhishek Bhattacharya**. 'Messily Married' is his second novel. His first novel 'Lollypops to Cigarettes' was published in October 2020.

Abhishek is a post-graduate in Business Management by education and a corporate leader by profession. Over the last two decades, he has been working with various multinationals and Indian firms. Abhishek has worked in leadership positions with Coca-Cola and PepsiCo in the past and presently associated with a large retail conglomerate based in Mumbai, India.

He has grown up in the city of Kolkata. His entire student life, from school to post-graduation, was completed in Kolkata. After that, during his tenures with various organisations, he has worked and lived in various cities in India.

Right from childhood, he has been passionate about literature and creative writing. His writing skills had won many accolades during his college days. He always had a deep desire to write and publish novels. For a long time, the wish was veiled by his corporate responsibilities. Finally, he could steal out time from packed schedules to publish his novel – 'Messily Married'.

For any feedback, Abhishek can be reached at

Email: ahattacharya36@gmail.com

LinkedIn: linkedin.com/in/abhishek-bhattacharya-442659198

Instagram: abhishek. bhattacharya.96

Chapter 1

A Sword Swaying Over Shreya

(July 2008)

21st July 2008, Fortis Hospital, Kandivali, Mumbai

It was Shreya's birthday, and this surely was not the place to celebrate it. I was waiting outside the ICU while Shreya lay on the other side of the green curtains.

'You are very late in getting her admitted,' said Doctor Kishori Kadam as she handed over a form to me for my signatures.

'A sword is swaying on her head, we will have to operate on her immediately,' added Doctor Kadam.

'Please sign the form and contact the billing desk to complete the formalities,' she said.

'Can I see her once doctor,' I asked?

She paused a while before replying, 'Well you can, but be short and quick. We have to get her ready for the operation immediately.'

I stepped in to see Shreya. I smiled at her but really did not know what to say. I did not have enough words to console her or even console myself. I stood beside her bed and held her hand. She was still sobbing, probably more due to her emotional rather than her physical pain. I wanted to hug her, but I resisted, as that may cause Shreya to break down with tears. We never thought our biggest dream of life will land us up in the ICU of the Fortis hospital. Neither of us even heard of ectopic pregnancy before.

'You are more important to me than anyone else Shreya,' I said.

'If you are with me, we can try once again to have a child. Let us get the foetus out of you quickly and head home happily. All I want is you to be safe and healthy again,' I told her.

Only four weeks ago, we literally jumped with joy inside our bathroom when we saw the two red stripes on the pregnancy test card. We hugged each other with joy. At last, our dream of a complete family was beginning to seem real. It had been five years since we got married in 2003. For the first four years, we were a happy-go-lucky couple and wanted some time for ourselves before we took the responsible step of becoming parents. After the very first year of marriage itself, our respective set of parents and relatives, like typical Indian relatives, had been pushing us to have a child. But we stayed strong on our goals and relentlessly pushed aside all advice about having a baby. Shreya and I were damn clear that the first four years of married life will be solely for the two of us. We had a bucket list to fulfill. Advance our respective careers, own a small house in Mumbai, buy a small car, have at least a couple of international and desi vacations, etc. A baby was not our immediate priority. So, we chased our dreams relentlessly, and quite successfully.

It was one year ago, in a gondola on the Venetian Canal that Shreya and I decided that we were ready to have a child in our lives. By then we had completed four successful and blissful years of marriage. It was on our fourth anniversary we decided to visit the city of love – Venice, Italy. On that chilly afternoon, on a Gondola, we locked our lips and hands as we floated around the most romantic city in the world. That's when Shreya spoke about it.

'Why don't we start saving money on condoms from now on, Abhi,' she said.

It took me a few seconds to gauge what she was hinting at.

'Is this the time to bring on this topic, Shreya?' I said.

'We are on a lovely anniversary vacation, why don't we think about it when we return to Mumbai?' I replied.

She remained silent for the rest of the gondola ride. It's not just Shreya, but I guess that's how most wives behave when their husband is not in line with their thoughts. We finished the gondola ride and were walking around the cold and narrow alleys of Venice. This time not holding hands, but in utter silence. I had to do something to get the mood back.

'Okay dear, if you are ready, then so am I,' I said.

'But consider that you have to bear most of the brunt as a mother,' I added.

'Are you ready to take a maternity break in your career, just when your career graph is steadily rising?' I tried to argue against her idea of having a baby.

Unlike most Indian men, I wanted my wife to excel in her career. I was truly happy when Shreya's pay cheque surpassed mine. I felt that it brought along huge financial security to the family. Now that she was rising on the corporate ladder, I did not want to put a break on her career because of this decision.

'Can't we wait for two more years, Shreya?' I asked.

'I don't believe that having a baby retards the career graph,' Shreya said after a long pause.

'Leave it to me to manage,' she said.

'My career will continue to demand my attention throughout my life, does it mean I will never become a mother?'

This was too logical a point for me to counter, I thought. Right through the evening till dinner, I went on at my attempts to convince her not to think of a baby right then. But I failed. At last, I relented. Probably she was right. In the last four years, we had almost ticked off all the items from the bucket list that we had kept for ourselves before having a baby. With a lot of effort and some luck, we were well poised in our respective jobs. I had moved on from Johnson Tiles, to become a Logistics Manager with Coca-Cola's largest bottling plant in India. Shreya moved on from her initial trainee job at Regal Logistics, to becoming a National Manager with Unilever. I had no qualms in proudly admitting that her pay cheque was fatter than mine. There was one financial rule we set for ourselves as a 'dink' couple – this rule held us back from comparing our pay cheques and live as a financially happy couple. We of course had separate salary accounts with Citi Bank, but we opened a joint account with ICICI bank. On the third day of every month, we transferred our previous month's salary into this joint account without fail. The money in the joint account was treated as 'our' money and lost its identity as Shreya's or mine. Hence there were no financial hard feelings between us. With the combined salaries of two managers of top multinationals, Shreya and my joint account was probably better than that of most of our peers. When many in our peer group were still struggling to board Mumbai local trains, we already possessed a bright red Suzuki Alto, we lived in a posh Mumbai high rise and already had two international vacations in four years. When our batchmates were counting money to pay rents, we had already had our own flat in Borivali.

The only aspect in which we lagged behind as compared to our peer groups was in having a bright son or daughter even after four years of our marriage. So ultimately, I relented to Shreya's decision to start a family. Once we returned to Mumbai after our Venetian vacation, I struck off condoms from being a part of my weekly grocery list. One thing I must secretly admit is that I was probably not the most sexually active hubby in town. There was no dearth in my love for Shreya, but somehow our sex lives had become a bit dull within a couple of years of our marriage. Neither of us complained though. Our respective jobs kept us busy during the weekdays. We almost had 12 to 13 hours of work time, including the drive through the crazy Mumbai traffic. Saturday mornings went in weekly grocery pickups, while evenings went in cinema halls, shopping malls, and booze parties. Sunday half days were usually spent on the bed with hangovers from Saturday night. It was mostly on Sunday afternoons or evenings when Shreya and I had the chance and inclination to do the do. We always used latex between us though. With the task on the hand of delivering a family, the latex went away but our sexual frequency remained the same. Instead of condoms, my shopping list now contained pregnancy test kits. Several months and several test kits went by, but the result was not how we wanted it to be. Eight months later, we got a bit worried – was something wrong with any of us? This was a worry which we could not openly discuss with our family and friends. But of course, we had a gynaecologist in our own family. Aarushi, my very own sister, was a practicing gynaecologist in Vancouver, Canada. That gave us the idea, why not see a gynaecologist in aamchi Mumbai.

Then entered Dr Shweta Nalawade in our life's story. We depended on her to give us a new life. We never realised that she would almost be taking away Shreya's life.

'You have a polycystic ovary,' she said when she inspected Shreya for the first time.

Dr Nalawade scribbled a few medicines for her. She also explained to us the entire life cycle of the female ovule. This was new knowledge to me. She explained why the 8th day to 18th day of the women's menstrual cycle was the most fertile period. So, the sperm had to time it right. Which meant that we had to be sexually active between the 8th and 18th day to give the sperm the highest possible window to meet the ovule. I came back from the doctor's visit with a sexual calendar. It was like setting my office outlook calendar with tasks and meetings. Our beautifully romantic love-making affair now became a calendar event. We literally hung a calendar on the wall beside our bed. In our busy schedules, it was impossible otherwise to count the 8th to 18th day of Shreya's cycle. We started marking the date when Shreya started her periods and then marked down the dates when we MUST have sex during the month. This calendar killed me with stress.

Sex became another goal that needed to be achieved during the month. It looked like my official calendar – count inventory on 16th and 30th; send monthly reports to Head Quarter on 5th; do a financial audit on 19th etc. etc. I started to feel the 'performance pressure' as the calendar dates came closer every month. I tried all sorts of ways, but I still could not perform on most of the days during the 8th to 18th-day cycle. I just could not relax my mind and the sperms refused to ooze out. First few months I struggled to sleep with my own wife. I tried all sorts of boosters to boost my performance – watching porn, skipping meetings to return home early, meditations to keep the mind under control. Nothing worked and the 'performance pressure' kept mounting on me. Initially, Shreya was amused at my plight every night. Then she became empathetic and tried to give me time to perform. Gradually she became irritated with my non-performance and that did not help me at all. Nonetheless, we kept on putting joint efforts between the 8th to 18th days of Shreya's menstrual cycle. The net result remained still the same – no result at all. Pregnancy cards kept on showing just one single red strand and got thrown in the dustbin.

Finally, on the last Sunday of May 2008, the pregnancy test kit showed two dark red strands. It announced the presence of another life inside Shreya. I could compare my sperms with the spider in the story of King Robert Bruce. After months of failure, my sperms had finally succeeded in creating a new life. Shreya and I jumped with joy inside our bathroom. We took leave from the office the next day and visited Dr Shweta Nalawade. She was like God to us.

'Thank you, doctor, now please show us the way to delivery,' I said

'The next step is to get a beta HCG test done so that we are absolutely sure of the pregnancy,' said Doctor Nalawade.

We were both shocked a bit. Our excitement about the baby died down instantly.

'Do you mean you are not sure that Shreya is pregnant?' I asked the doc.

'The external urine test kits are not the surest pregnancy test, Abhinav. Moreover, it also does not proclaim the stage of the pregnancy. So, to know the exact stage of the foetus we need to do a blood test which is called the beta HCG test,' explained Doctor Nalawade.

So, blood was drawn out of Shreya's veins to check the beta count. If the beta count is over 25 mlU/ml then the pregnancy was certain, we learned. Unfortunately, the test result would come only in the evening, meaning a good seven hours later. This was probably the beginning of anxious hours that Shreya and I spent during her short-lived pregnancy. We had taken the day off from the office and had to kill these seven hours somehow. We had a quick grub in a small South Indian Udupi joint just off the doctor's clinic. In our excitement, we had eaten nothing since morning, and now in our anxiousness, we could hardly finish a dosa each. We then decided to proceed to a nearby multiplex and catch on to a movie to distract our anxious minds. We did buy tickets and get into the theatre, but we hardly registered anything in the movie, including its name and star cast. Right through the movie I had been watching my watch. I stepped out twice to call up the clinic and ask if Shreya Bhattacharya's beta report was ready. Finally, we went back to the clinic and checked her beta report. That was probably the best report card that I had seen in my life till then, the beta count showed 30 mlU/ml. Yes, Shreya was pregnant! We hugged each other.

It was my happiest moment in life. I literally felt like dancing a jig. We came home with the report, grinning all the way. On the way home, I bought a bottle of damn expensive champagne. We burst open the cork moments after we reached home. Of course, Shreya had only one sip. She had to be out of alcohol for the next one year for sure. So, I finished the whole bottle with glee. I felt like calling the whole world and letting them know that I am going to be a father in nine months. But Shreya stopped me. As per her, for the first few months, this is supposed to stay a secret from the larger world. We never thought that keeping this a secret would land us up in serious trouble. We at least should have told our parents and Aarushi, who was a gynaecologist. We could have surely got better guidance from her than Dr Shweta Nalawade. Her negligence was the cause of the sword swaying over Shreya's head today.

Two nurses interjected my thoughts. I was asked to leave the ICU as the nurses had to prepare Shreya for immediate surgery. I left Shreya's hand and slowly left the room. I stood outside the ICU, all alone. I wished I had spoken about Shreya's pregnancy to some close friends at least. I could have had some moral support now. The only person in the world who knew about Shreya's ectopic pregnancy was Aarushi. Tough she was miles away in Vancouver, it was her medical judgment that suspected that Shreya's pregnancy was not normal but ectopic. But it was way too late to save Shreya from danger. How I wished I spoke to Aarushi sooner. We should not have hidden Shreya's pregnancy from our own family. How I regret it now, but time cannot be undone.

Our biggest dream of life was shattered as Shreya was wheeled through the corridor on her journey to the operation theatre. She smiled at me as she passed by. I tried to smile back at her but couldn't. I followed her to the entrance of the OT. This is where we had to part. I could feel my eyes moisten once again. I never felt so alone and helpless. Dr Kishori Kadam walked up to me.

'Pray for her,' she said with a smile. The OT gates shut on me, with Shreya on the other side.

———

Chapter 2

LIFE IN THE FIFTH GEAR

(February 2003)

'Did you enjoy screwing Maria that night?' asked Shashi.

'Is this the right time to talk about it,' I stared at him?

'Look who is embarrassed,' grinned Chirag.

'Hope you have invited Shreelekha. It would be great to see your first girlfriend attending your first marriage,' taunted Shashi.

Shashi, Chirag, and I were crammed into the back seat of a Maruti Esteem car. I was all decked up as the groom and sitting in the middle, crushed from both sides by my dear friends Shashi and Chirag. Shashi was on my left and Chirag on the right. On the front seat was the driver and beside the driver sat a puny-looking, thin, ill-clad gentleman, who had come to fetch me to my marriage venue. Yes, I was getting married to Shreya today. As per Bengali customs, the girl's family had to send a saloon car, decorated with flowers, to fetch the groom from his house to the bride's house. The ceremony of marriage was conducted in the bride's house. The next day, post marriage, the same car (with flowers already withered) dropped the bride and groom together back to the groom's place. Keeping up to the custom, Mr Ghosh – Shreya's father, had sent this Esteem, all decorated with red roses and equipped with a driver and an accomplice, to fetch me from my house to his house for the wedding ceremony. This is the one ride that every Bengali man dreams of having someday. I was no different. At every red signal that we stopped on, people from other cars, buses, and scooters peeped into our car to have a glimpse of me – the groom. I felt like a hero on that day. I feel amused at the inquisitiveness of Bongs. Every person on the road was interested to see how the groom and bride looked. In fact, I was no different and behaved the same way when I was on the other side. I too have peeped into so many decorated saloon cars to have a glimpse of the newlyweds. But today I knew how it felt to be sitting inside the decked-up car, all dressed up with others peeping into my personal space.

'Hey Chirag, hope you have organised the booze for tonight,' asked Shashi

'Of course, man, it is our best friend's wedding and booze shall be oozing out of everywhere,' said Chirag, as he pulled out a nip of dark rum from the inner pocket of his jacket.

'What the fuck, are you guys going to start off right here in the car?' I said, grossly annoyed at the idea.

'Want to try?' said Chirag while taking a sip from the bottle and handing it over to Shashi.

'Are you out of your minds? Drinking is completely taboo in Bengali marriages and that too by the groom himself.' I said.

'In fact, the bride and groom are expected to be fasting on this day, till the marriage is over', I added.

'That's good. You keep to your dieting, while we can finish the bottle,' said Shashi, passing the bottle back to Chirag, right under my nose. The smell of dark rum made me salivate a little. I just love rum and coke.

'Hope you guys have more bottles reserved for the night. I am just waiting for the marriage ceremony to be over and then I shall celebrate my marriage in my own style,' I grinned.

'Don't worry mate, I have a bottle of Johnny and a pint of Captain Cook in my bag,' said Chirag.

'We will drench you so much tonight that Shreya will be saved from getting fucked on the very first night,' laughed Shashi

That's what friends are for. I am so thankful to have friends like these. Shashi had flown in from Mumbai this afternoon while Chirag had crossed three continents and flown down from Boston just to attend my wedding. I was sure Shashi would keep my invitation, but honestly, I never thought that one simple email invitation will pull Chirag all the way from Boston to Kolkata, to witness me getting married to Shreya. And he gave me the surprise in style. He did not tell me that he is going to come. He reached my house, wanting to give me a surprise. He saw the decorated car waiting outside to take me to Shreya's place. He quietly sneaked in it and waited in the car. Even when I was getting in the car, along with Shashi, I had no clue that it was Chirag who was sitting in the back seat. I thought it would be one of Shreya's relatives who had come to fetch me. When I looked up at his face, I could not believe my eyes!

'You bastard, you never told me you will come,' I said, visibly overjoyed.

'I am sorry mate, I could not bring a gift for you on your marriage, I had no money left after paying for the return air fare from Boston to Kolkata,' grinned Chirag.

'Your presence is my biggest gift, you rascal,' I said, hugging Chirag

For the rest of the journey, we three musketeers kept on jabbering about our good old days. We used to be flatmates during our bachelor days. There was another guy along with us, Pradip. The four of us bachelor boys worked for Johnson Tiles in Mumbai and lived together in a two-bedroom flat in Kalyan. At the office, we were well known as 'the fantastic four'. We hailed from different cities and destiny had thrown us together in our first job in the commercial capital of India. Right through the journey in the back seat of the car, we kept talking about our days in Kalyan. The bars we visited, the adventures we had, the beers we gulped down, and of course the time we spent in the infamous dance bars of Mumbai.

'You remember the day we got picked up from a dance bar by the Mulund police?' reminded Shashi.

I laughed out loud at the memory. 'Of course, it was all because of this bastard,' I said, pointing out to Chirag.

'Yes,' agreed Shashi. 'Had he not wanted to go into the Chandi bar at 3 AM that morning, we would not have landed into the lock-up.'

'It's all an experience bhai, had I not made all of us see the inside of a lock-up for the first time,' Chirag smiled.

'Hopefully the last time too,' I smiled back.

'You did not answer my question, did you enjoy the fuck with Maria?' Shashi asked me again.

Maria was the hooker who Shashi had arranged for me in a hotel room in Mumbai the night before I was scheduled to fly down to Kolkata for my marriage. That's was his marriage gift to me.

'She was the fuck of the century man. I enjoyed your gift, thanks Shashi,' I said.

The three of us laughed out loud.

'Wasn't that going a bit too far, that too on the night before your marriage?' The words came from an unknown voice.

Shashi, Chirag, and I looked at each other, then looked up at the front seat towards the speaker of the last words.

All the while we were talking, we paid no heed to the puny stranger sitting in the front seat, beside the driver, and eavesdropping into our stories, smiling from time to time. He was probably one of the typical accomplices that my father-in-law would have sent to fetch me from my house, I presumed. Probably too unimportant a character to have paid any attention to. But when he spoke again, I could feel my throat dry up.

'Hello gentlemen, I am Swarup Ghosh, Shreya's uncle, and Mr Ghosh's younger brother', he said waving at us.

Pin drop silence prevailed in the back seat. Now, this uncle-in-law knew every damn chapter of my book written during my bachelorhood. Holy shit. If Shreya's father comes to know that I have been hooking up with Maria the night before my marriage and today I have drunk friends accompanying me to the marriage, then there are high chances that the ceremony would get cancelled.

'We have almost arrived. It shall take another five minutes. All the best,' said Swarup Ghosh looking at me.

I kept a straight face. For the rest of the journey, none of us spoke. The only sounds were a few beeps from Shashi's and my cell phone as we kept exchanging text messages.

'Make sure Mr. Swarup Ghosh does not see my father-in-law till the marriage ceremony is over,' I texted Shashi.

'How do I recognise your father-in-law,' he replied.

'The first man to whom I shall bow down and touch feet of would-be my father-in-law, that's the signal you will take to act.' I messaged.

'Sure, how do I prevent them from meeting, should I kidnap Swarup and thrust our dark rum bottle down his throat,' texted Shashi.

'Fucker, don't joke now, every time you see them getting close, distract one of them by asking silly questions.' I texted back.

'What silly questions?'

'Anything, such as where is the toilet, how old is the house, how many guests are coming... blah blah, blah.' I texted as the car came to a halt in front of Shreya's house.

This is where my life would shift into the fifth gear, I thought as I stepped out of the car and crossed the main door into Shreya's house. When I come out of this gate again, I shall be a married man. I will lose my bachelor's degree in this house this evening. One must know that crossing the gates of the bride's house on the day of marriage is not as easy for the groom as it seems to be. There are a host of ceremonies to be performed. There was an 'aarti' done by the mother-in-law while I stood with a straight face. There were loads of unknown fancy female faces looking at me and giggling for no reason. In my last hour of bachelorhood, my eyes should have feasted on these well-decked bong beauties, but instead all the while my eyes revolved to find Swarup Ghosh and ensure that he was not meeting Swapan Ghosh, my father in law. I could see Shashi hovering just behind Swarup Ghosh. I felt assured by seeing that Shashi had his man marked well, just like a defender marks the opponent striker in a soccer game. Nonetheless, with a lot of fanfare, I entered the house and waited in a lavishly decorated room for the marriage ceremony to begin.

All through my growing up years, I had seen so many Bengali marriage ceremonies. They were really elaborate. There is one aspect I found very typical and mystical about Bengali marriages. The bride is well decked up in a red 'Baranasi' saree with gold ornaments covering as much skin as the bride's father can afford. The groom, on the other hand, is dressed in a dhoti and banyan only. He is not even allowed to wear a decent kurta. To add to it, he wears a very odd-shaped funny-looking head gear called 'topor'. I wondered why the poor groom is robbed of the kurta off his back right when he is getting married. Probably symbolic of what is going to happen to him for the rest of his life. I was no exception. I was escorted to the cynosure of the ceremony, dressed in a dhoti (which I somehow managed to hold together at the right place) and just an inner wear banyan. It was early February and still cold in Kolkata and this was not the most comfortable attire for sure. Luckily there was a fire burning right in the middle of the thoroughfare which gave me some comfort from the cold.

In the next two hours, a lot of incomprehensible Sanskrit slokas went on being uttered by an old priest in our journey to be proclaimed as a couple. I was enjoying being the cynosure of attention of the crowd around. Shreya sat beside me in her red saree, the 'pallu' covering her face. Even with the veil, she looked magical to me today. Her red saree and gold jewellery made her shine like a Hindu Goddess. Even with so many other bong beauties around me, I could not take my eyes off her. At one point in time, the priest gave vermilion in my hand and asked me to apply the same on Shreya's head. I lifted Shreya's pallu thus unveiling her beautiful face. I looked at her directly for the first time this evening. There were streaks of sweat on her forehead, probably caused due to covering it for so long. Her evergreen eyes and mesmerising smile stood as they were. I gradually lifted my hand and put the vermillion on her forehead. By Hindu customs, we were officially married now. Life had changed to its fifth gear - from here on it would either be full speed ahead or reverse gear. Time would only tell.

During the rest of the ceremony, Shreya and I had to perform more customary procedures of a bong marriage. We exchanged our garlands among loud cheers from the crowd. All these years I had been a part of the crowd and today I was on the other end of the table. Though, out of sheer habit, I also started cheering my own garland exchanges. Then we were asked to go around the fire in circles. This part I loved as it made me recall numerous Hindi film marriage scenes. After the ceremonies were done, Shreya and I were escorted over to a dais where we sat side by side welcoming numerous relatives and guests. Thank God, I was, at last, offered a decent enough kurta to wear over my innerwear. It was probably only on my marriage evening that I realised the number of relatives I had inherited. I was brought up in a nuclear family and had never realised the expanse of my family tree before. I had lost my father five years ago and thereafter knew only my mother and sister Aarushi as my close ones. But today plethora of uncles, aunties, first cousins, and eleventh cousins came and congratulated Shreya and me. The worst part was, every stranger asked me the same question, 'Do you recognise me?' – which of course I did not. But that evening, this one question asked many times over had taught me to master a magnificent skill. And that was how to give the right length of smile with the right angle of nod which can be either a 'no' or and 'yes' to the question. It would then be left to the eyes of the beholder to interpret it to their liking. The meet and greet was followed by a sumptuous dinner which all and sundry, including me, looked forward to and enjoyed.

As the night progressed, the guest list was slowly packing off post the thirteen-course dinner. Gradually only the blood relations and very close friends were left over. Shreya and I were taken to a room to rest after the most eventful evening of our lives. There is another interesting twist in the bong marriage customs. God only knows why, but the newly married couple is not left alone on the first night after marriage. They are to be surrounded by very close friends and siblings and are supposed to stay awake on the first night. Probably, the fathers-in-law do not approve of their daughters having sex in his house. Nonetheless, I found Shashi and Chirag already in the room when Shreya and I entered. Since our car ride here, I saw these two souls for the first time this evening. Luckily, Shashi had managed well to mark Swarup Ghosh closely and prevented him from reaching the goal post – I mean my father-in-law. Finally, the marriage ceremony was complete, and Shashi could let off his guard. From the smell of rum from their breaths, it seemed that Shashi and Chirag had already let off their guards.

'What do you want to try bhai, Captain Cook or Johnny Walker?' asked Chirag as we entered the room.

Drinking is fully taboo in all Bengali marriages, more so in the Ghosh household. So, a lot of secrecy had to be maintained before we uncorked the bottles. But that was not a problem at all. Chirag was an expert in such games. A coke bottle was half-filled with Captain cook while a soda bottle was diluted with whisky. We maintained limited access into the room and bolted it from inside. Apart from us, the new entrants to the night party were Dipankar, Shreya's best friend during her college days, Aarushi my sister, and Karan, Aarushi's husband. The six of us drank off a bottle of whisky and a pint of rum through the night. Shreya of course did not touch the liquor. Memories of each of our golden past whipped across the room for the rest of the night. Of course, we had taken a lesson from our afternoon experience in the car and so Maria's story was kept under the carpet.

Gradually dawn broke. The first rays of the sun fell on my face, waking me for the first time as a married man. All of us had dozed off by early morning. I was the first one to regain my senses. I found Shreya lying on my lap. Though I had kissed her, several times before as my girlfriend, for the first time I kissed my wife. The morning sun rays proclaimed the beginning of a fresh chapter in the lives of Mr and Mrs Bhattacharya. As I locked my lips with Shreya's little did I know, that within a decade of our marriage, these lips will lock less and talk more……

———

Chapter 3

Mumbai Masala

(October 2004)

Shreya and I were sipping banana shake from the same glass with two different straws, while our heads stuck together over the glass. One may think that's a very common romantic scene, right out of films. Well, so it was! But Shreya and I had been following this romantic gesture over the last few months, so much so that this had almost become a habit. Shreya and I reached the Borivali station in Mumbai almost at the same time after office, though from different directions. I travelled back to Borivali from the Coca-Cola plant in Vasai where I work, while she travelled from her Kodak office in Santacruz. We met at the Borivali station every evening and then we shared a milkshake from the same glass, before walking back home to Raheja Gardens, Borivali. No matter who reached the Borivali station first waited for the other. I had started this practice just after we shifted to Mumbai post our marriage. We have held up this practice ever since.

In fact, as per Shreya, I am a very romantic husband. That sure is a big accolade to possess for any Indian husband. Of course, I worked towards getting that feather on my cap. The very first day Shreya flew with me to Mumbai from Kolkata after our wedding, I had organized a saloon car to pick us up at the domestic airport. That was not all, the chauffer of the car was waiting with a pre-organised large bouquet of white and red roses, which was handed over to Shreya as soon as we came out of the airport security. And then, when Shreya opened the rear door of the saloon, she jumped with pleasant shock. The entire rear seat was covered with chocolates and candies. All of these were organized by me through Shashi. Shashi was back in Mumbai after our marriage well before us, while Shreya and I spent another week in the Puri sea beach on our honeymoon. I had planned the brilliant reception for Shreya and asked Shashi to get all this organised. From that very moment, when Shreya stepped into Mumbai, I had earned my distinction of being a very romantic husband.

Our romantic journey continued while Shreya was settling down in the new city and newly married life. Though I had been living in Mumbai for the last three years, it was Shreya's first brush with the city. The initial days in Mumbai, for any newcomer, become a bit tough to digest. But when it comes to being in a relationship with Mumbai, two months is a good enough time to decide which way it would go. Some fall in love with the city in these two months and resolve not to leave forever, while some detest it and start looking for a way out. Luckily both Shreya and I fell into the first category. We enjoyed the masala of Mumbai and wanted to achieve our goals in this city. While I had arranged Shreya's reception into Mumbai with flowers and chocolates, Mumbai gifted us both with an accelerated job change very soon after we arrived in her lap as a couple – as if it was a marriage gift to us. Within five months, both of us moved into our new companies. While I moved out of Johnson tiles to join Coca-Cola, Shreya resigned from Regal Logistics to join Kodak. From that time till now, every evening we dated at the Borivali station with a shared milkshake and then walked back to our abode hand-in-hand. The romance had already begun getting converted into a habit.

Life was moving well in Mumbai. Prosperity gradually crept in as days moved on. The economic potential of a DINK (double income no kids) couple was taking shape, and we bought our first car even before we completed our first year of marriage. In December 2003, on Christmas Day, we purchased our first Maruti Alto with a down payment of Rs. 50,000 and a monthly EMI of 5000. I had just learned driving a few months ago and was still a novice. My heart was trembling as I drove out of the Kandivali Suzuki showroom with our new red Alto. Even though we gleamed with our achievement to buy our first car, our dreams did not stop there. Dare to dream was our motto – more Shreya's than mine. She really possessed the courage to dream big. We barely settled in with our Alto and she already had an Audi in mind. From an Alto to an Audi in fifteen years was the target that we set for ourselves. Pretty ambitious for sure, but only time would tell, I thought.

A new car naturally called for a celebration. More so because our friends forced us for a party. The next weekend, our humble two-bed apartment was filled with friends, fun, and frolic. Shashi was of course there, along with his fiancée Shalini. A couple of my colleagues from Coca-Cola joined in and so did some of Shreya's colleagues from Kodak. The evening was going on well with whisky, vodka, chicken, and laughter doing the rounds. I personally felt very pleased with the fact that we had bought our first car. But one secret to the happiness I realised that evening. The fact that I was the first one among the group of friends in the room to own a car made me feel happier than the fact that I had just bought a car. I learned that happiness lay in being more successful than your peers. I also realised that very few people, including me, get sincerely pleased with their neighbour's prosperity. In fact, the easiest way to unhappiness was a comparison. The one who celebrates the other's success from the heart is a true friend. The rest are just fair-weather friends. Who among the group of nine people qualify to be 'true friends'? I asked myself. Probably I will know some day when the weather is not this fair.

Time moved on. Shreya and I were well settled in our new jobs in Kodak and Coca-Cola respectively. Since we held the same post-graduate degree from the same post-graduate college, the nature of our jobs and designations were also similar. Shreya was the West Region Logistics Manager for Kodak and I held the exact same title for Coca-Cola. (For the benefit of readers who did not read about how we met in my first story- *Lollypops to Cigarettes*, I would take a pause here and recapitulate a bit.) Shreya and I studied our post-graduation in Logistics Management from the same institution, IISWBM Kolkata. Shreya was a year junior to me in the two-year course. Though we knew each other in college, we did not have a romantic relationship. We just did our 'hi and hello' when we crossed paths and very occasionally caught up for coffee at the college canteen. How we landed up in tying up in a marital knot is a novel by itself (Refer to my book- *Lollypops to Cigarettes*). It was one fine evening, in Nolbon Kolkata that we met after a year of finishing our post-graduation. I was already working in Johnson Tiles in Mumbai by that time and was on a vacation in Kolkata. Shreya had just graduated from IISWBM and cracked a campus interview with Regal Logistics. Her job assignment was also in Mumbai and so she had contacted me to do some research on the city. That's how we decided to catch up that evening in Nolbon, Kolkata.

I don't know why Shreya chose Nolbon as a meeting point to discuss her new job in Mumbai. For those who are not privy to Kolkata, Nolbon is a lover's paradise and not an ideal place for a professional discussion. Nolbon is a park with a large lake where couples can hire a paddleboat, get to the centre of the lake, and make the best use of the privacy.

On the day of the meeting, I reached first. Though I had a cell phone at that time, Shreya did not. Hence, I had no option but to wait at the pre-agreed meeting point – the solitary café inside Nolbon. I kept staring at the lake in a daze as I sipped on to the cold coffee I ordered in the café. I could see the lake dotted with multi-coloured paddle boats. Every boat had a couple seated so close to each other that it was hard to tell which was the male and which was the female from this distance. All the boats had their face turned away from the café side of the lake. I could just see two heads held tightly together, leaving nothing to the imagination that the two sets of lips would be intertwined on the other side of the two heads. By the time I finished my second helping of cold coffee, Shreya had come and sat next to me. I probably saw her after two years. That day was probably the first time I gave a long look at Shreya. A typical Bengali female prototype: plump on the hips and breasts, extremely fair in complexion, and with a goddess-like face backed by a million-dollar smile. In short, a true bong beauty, who would make a lovely candidate for a matrimonial alliance. No, even at that point, I had no intention of making her my bride, and so to say marriage was not at all on my cards – I was just twenty-five and had had sex only with two partners so far. I sure looked forward to more daring affairs before settling down as a loyal Bengali hubby.

While I was all prepared to carry out the conversation at the café itself on a couple of more coffees, Shreya, to my surprise, wanted to talk on a paddleboat. Without any hesitation, I relented. We hired a boat for two hours at the rate of a hundred rupees an hour and very soon found ourselves somewhere deep inside the lake, far away from any third set of eyes. We started a professional conversation.

'How is Mumbai as a city to live in alone? Are you enjoying it?' she asked.

Like, how I researched about Mumbai before I went there two years ago, she was trying to do the same. She had found out from friends around that I was working in Mumbai, hunted out my cell phone number, and voila, we are together in the middle of Nolbon Lake having this conversation.

'To be honest, it took me some time to adjust to the city, but once I settled in, I felt it was the best place to be in; it is indeed the city of dreams,' I said.

'But of course, you will have to keep your 'bangaliana' back in Calcutta before you head to Mumbai. It is a city for true hard workers and not for the typical bongs who love jhal muri, phuchka et al.,' I added with a smile.

'What about the cost of living there? How safe is it for a single girl?' she inquired.

'Mumbai is a city where one can live with any budget – from a mere five thousand a month to a five lakh a month. One has to make one's own choice,' I replied.

'According to all the statistics, it is the safest city in India for women,' I assured her.

A few more tits and bits on each other's job, family, and Mumbai followed through in our conversation. I spoke about my days in Johnson tiles, the fantastic four, about how I still missed Dad. She spoke about her first campus interview, on Regal Logistics being the leading Cargo player of Asia, about her family – her mom, dad, and younger brother. Our conversation lasted for more than an hour, and by that time, the sun had started gradually setting on the lake. We both stopped our conversation and relished the sunset as the dusk was setting in on the city of joy. The red sun was gradually tilting towards the lake, making its reflection on the still waters. It looked as if two suns were coming closer and closer to kiss each other goodbye. Our tongues stopped, and our eyes looked up to the lake, and soon the two sets of eyes looked at one another. I still don't know how it started. I truly did not intend to consciously. But we found our four lips together and the two tongues intermingled for God knew how much time. As we paddled our boat back towards the Café at the shore, the setting sun god probably had locked our fates to go on paddling together to the next phase of life. The rest was history. Soon our families met and decided to tie us up in the marital knot. In exactly five months from our meeting in Nolbon, Shreya and I got married.

To date, I falter to answer the question about our marriage being a love marriage or an arranged one. Nonetheless, our first year of marriage was filled with romantic moments for sure. We enjoyed each other's company. We gave each other surprise gifts, we went to movies on weekends, went for long drives on rainy afternoons. In fact, on one such long drive, we were lip-locking as we drove and were caught by the cops. That was an embarrassing moment for us. The cops who caught us, for some reason, refused to believe that Shreya was my legal wife. Marathi cops had no idea that married couples could have lip locks outside of their bedrooms. How could I prove that Shreya was my wife? Naturally, we would not carry our passports or marriage certificate on a drive. But with their experience, they did know how to test actual marital bonds. I was asked to step out of the car, to which I abided. One cop walked with me a few meters and asked me my marriage date. '2nd February 2003,' I said confidently, not knowing what soup I landed myself in. The cop then walked back to the car where Shreya was still sitting and asked her the same question. 3rd Feb 2003, she gave the right marriage date. Fuck! How could I forget my marriage date right at that time! Naturally, the two cops were not convinced at all and were all set to charge us with PDA and adultery. Luckily, owing to my nature of work at Coca-Cola, I happened to know the local SP of police who helped me bail out of the situation without any charges.

We did have occasional tiffs now and then. Most of these were related to my habit of smoking. Though Shreya had somewhat compromised to agree to my weekend drinking spree, she was a real nagger when it came to my smoking. But I just could not kick the butt. Probably there was not enough urge to. But I did bring it down from ten sticks a day to six. As much as possible, I stopped smoking after I reached home so that I can avoid the nagging from my wife. But the biggest fight happened when Shreya wanted to leave Kodak and join Unilever in Belapur, Navi Mumbai.

'So, you are no different from the typical Indian man who is jealous of his wife's success,' she accused me.

Unilever gave her a good offer for sure. It was almost an 80% jump over her current Kodak compensation and way above my compensation in Coca-Cola. Moreover, it was a National Manager's position. But trust me, I was happy with it. I always wanted her to flourish in her career and did not at all mind if she surpassed me. But I found it hard to explain that to her.

'Trust me Shreya, I am very proud of you that you could crack through a firm like Unilever,' I said.

'Then what is the issue?' Why do you want me to reject the offer?' She asked.

'It is just because of the distance of their office. Belapur is far off from Borivali,' I tried to explain.

And it indeed was. Belapur was almost 50 kilometres from where we stayed, and it would require three local train changes to go there.

'You cannot manage to change three crowded locals to reach office, then work for a full day and return with three trains again. It would be taxing for you Shreya,' I tried to explain to her.

'I will manage,' she replied.

'How will you manage all the cooking and washing after you come back from the office, you will be too tired,' I tried to reason

'There you go, typical male chauvinist. Is a post-graduate woman married to you for cooking and washing?' Shreya snarled at me.

'Don't get me wrong, I am just concerned about your own comfort than your career,' I reasoned.

'To me, my career is more important than anything else,' Shreya shouted back.

That did it, I lost my mind. I picked up a glass from the dining table and threw it at Shreya. The glass hit her on the knee, and she wailed in pain while sitting down on the floor.

'You stay with your bright career then,' I yelled.

The next moment in raging anger I left the house banging the door behind me. I took the lift to the lobby and headed out of the building.

As I walked aimlessly in the crowded Borivali streets, I tried to reason my anger. How did I throw the glass at Shreya? How much did her knee hurt or was she just acting to get my sympathy? Shit! What would have happened if the glass hit her on the face or head? I shivered at the thought. How could I throw the glass at her? But she too did not understand my logic at all. How can she think her career was the most important thing to her? I tried to justify my anger in my own thoughts as I kept on walking the streets in the late summer evening. Shreya failed to understand why I was insisting not to take up the job with Unilever. I was more possessive and protective than career-oriented. She would not understand that I just stopped her so that she does not take the pain of traveling 100 kilometres every day. I was never concerned that she had a better job than mine. I was just concerned about the hardship that she would have to face to do this job. We could shift to Belapur, but that would mean I travel almost 200 kilometres every day up and down from Belapur to Vasai and back. In our current set up we were logistically right in staying exactly equidistant from both our offices. She would never understand – I thought.

The night was deepening, and I felt very hungry. We started the fight just before dinner and we both had not eaten anything since our evening banana shake. Shreya disclosed her decision just as we were settling for our dinner and then this brawl happened. Slowly my anger within was also softening. I was feeling massively guilty for hitting my dear sweet wife with a glass. I headed back home. As I entered our dark flat, I could not see Shreya. I called out to her as I switched on the lights. I checked both bedrooms and

I could not find her. I started to feel worried. Did she also leave after I left? I tried calling her on her phone. The phone rang and it was still lying on the living room sofa. She had not carried the phone with her. What do I do? Where do I look for her? I felt so sorry for hitting her like that. Couldn't I have been a more understanding partner? I knew full well that Shreya was an ambitious girl. Whether I liked it or not, her career would be her priority. We could have worked out a solution. Probably we could stay somewhere mid-way between Belapur and Vasai. Probably with her new inflated pay cheque, she could spend on a chauffeur and drive to Belapur and not have to change crowded local trains. Solutions would have emerged if I was more understanding. Tears rolled down my eyes as I remembered throwing a glass at Shreya. My thoughts seized as I entered the washroom to wash my tears. Shreya lay on the bathroom floor, sobbing softly. Her knee was wrapped in a towel while blood was dripping from it. She withered in pain as I touched her knee. She needed medical attention immediately.

It was well past midnight when everything was settled, and we could come out of Suraksha Hospital in Borivali West. I hugged Shreya for how she had saved me from sheer embarrassment at the hospital. The administrative staff at the Suraksha Hospital refused to believe that Shreya had accidentally slipped and fallen on a piece of glass. Shreya had come up with that story, else it would have been a clear police case against me for domestic violence. Shreya somehow managed to convince the staff that it was an accident, though the nurses and the doctor clearly eyed me with a lot of malice and doubt. An X-ray was taken on Shreya's knee and luckily nothing had broken. She was released with a dressing of the wound and a pain killer injection. The doctor advised her to rest the knee for seven days. I supported her as she slowly walked out of the hospital.

'I am really sorry dear, I promise it will never happen again,' I told her.

'You can work for Unilever and we shall hire a driver to drive you to the office every day. Cheers to your new career madam,' I smiled at Shreya.

'That's good, I shall carry vegetables and chop them in the car itself so that I can get dinner cooked immediately as I reach home,' she smiled back at me.

I hugged her tight. That was probably the boldest and best decision that Shreya took which kept on paying well for the rest of her career. Life moved on for us into a better tomorrow.

———

Chapter 4

WATER WATER EVERYWHERE

(July 2005)

Memories were crossing past my mind as I sat on top of the car. The water level was rising very fast. The rain had not seized, though the intensity had reduced. Passing thoughts of all my life's events were grieving me more and more. Will I ever see Shreya again? Will I be able to get to my cosy bedroom with her? Will I be able to return to Kolkata to meet mom for one last time? All these thoughts prowled across my mind. I sobbed as loudly as I could. Apart from my driver, Maqbul, there was no other living being close enough to hear me cry. I remembered I read this somewhere. When one faces a near-death experience, one's whole life flashes in front of their eyes in no time. I was experiencing the same as I sat still on the top of the Toyota Qualis van. Flood waters sped past me. It was difficult to believe that I was stuck on the roof of a car on the busy Western Express Highway of Mumbai city. It felt like the car was stuck in the middle of a torrential river. Water was gushing through the main road. Maqbul and I sat still on top of the car, shivering in fear and cold. We were each other's Man Friday in this time of distress.

'Let's head back to Andheri and then sit over a drink, what say?' I asked Amit.

'Nope. Let's fill our tanks here in Vasai itself. The Sai Pranay Bar is much cheaper than drinking in any bar in Andheri,' replied Amit.

'That's right boss, they give the Coca-Cola fellas a heavy discount too,' added Yogesh.

'So be it,' I said, as the three musketeers head straight for the Sai Pranay Bar, which was right opposite to the plant in Vasai.

Amit, Yogesh, and I were popularly known as the three supply chain musketeers of Coca-Cola West Zone. While I was stationed at the Coca-Cola plant in Vasai, Amit and Yogesh were my allies in the Coca-Cola Regional office in Andheri. Though we were in hourly touch over phone and e mail, once or twice a month we met officially when they visited the plant, or I visited the region office. That was of course talking of official meetings only and not counting the numerous unofficial meetings we had during our movie and beer binge sessions. Today was one of those official meetings which invariably ended up in the nearest bar. Today, I was suggesting we head to Andheri and then drink so that we can head home right when we finished. But they did have a point. The

Sai Pranay did give employees good discounts since it was situated right opposite our plant. Drinking in Andheri would be a costlier option.

By the time we finished our first round of drinks, news had flown in about torrential rains hitting the city of Mumbai. Someone from the Andheri office had called and told us that. Apparently, streets were flooded, trains had been stopped, and traffic had come to a halt. We looked out of the small windows of the bar. Well, it was raining for sure but did not sound as intense as the caller was talking about. Still, I felt we ought head straight homewards.

'Come on Abhi', said Amit. 'It's the end of July, it will rain in Mumbai anyways. Let's not spill our drinks over it.'

'Yes sir. Mumbaikars invariably start panicking just on a bit of heavy rain. That's in our nature,' added Yogesh.

'Don't panic. Let's call for our next round of rum. This is the right climate for rum and coke, my friend,' Amit smiled and reached out for his glass.

Just to reassure me, I called Shreya to find out the state of Mumbai.

'Hello,' Shreya answered the call.

'Where are you, not in the office?' I asked as I heard immense noise in the background as Shreya answered the call.

Luckily Shreya did not go to the Belapur office that day. She was called for a meeting in the Unilever HQ in Andheri, which was much nearer to our home.

'I have already left from the head office. My colleague Lata and I are heading home in an auto-rickshaw'.

'What! So early? It's only 4 PM.' I said, surprised to find her on her way home.

'It's raining really badly in Mumbai, so everyone in the head office left home early. Others had left at 2 PM, Lata and I had some chores to finish and we left half an hour ago.'

'Where have you guys reached' I enquired?

'We are still on the Goregaon flyover. There is a lot of traffic and water is gushing through the highway. It may take two hours to reach home,' yelled Shreya as she spoke over the street noise in the background.

'Ok. Reach home and call me to let me know you reached safely,' I answered.

'Where are you? You also leave immediately. Trains from Vasai may stop anytime?' said Shreya.

'Don't worry about me. Amit and Yogesh are here at the plant and they came in an official vehicle. We shall leave in the same vehicle and I can duck the trains today.' I replied.

'Still. Don't delay. Hop in the car and head home. It's a nice rainy evening and we can have a romantic candlelight dinner. Love you, bye.'

'Shreya and her weird romantic ideas,' I thought.

'Bye. Love you too. Reach home and call me,' I hung up.

I told Amit and Yogesh that people in Mumbai were heading home and we too should start off immediately.

'Take a chill pill pal. One more round and we shall shoot home. We have a Toyota with us today and not your little Maruti, we will wade past the water with ease,' Yogesh concluded.

Though in double minds, I sat back on the table and ordered some more rum and coke. Spirits, they say, can lift your spirit. Whoever said this was bloody damn right! Two more pegs of black rum ran down my blood vessels and gave me immense strength to load two more pegs. We were completely oblivious to what nature had in store for us in Mumbai. At last, we started from Vasai to Mumbai at 7 PM in the evening.

'Let's go Maqbul, let's fly to Mumbai,' I said to the driver. I was already flying high in spirits.

Shreya would be home by now, we spoke three hours ago I thought. I took out my cell and dialled her number. The call did not go through, all networks on the route are jammed – said an auto-recorded female voice. Damn. I tried from Amit's phone, but the result was the same. Amit tried calling Cynthia, his wife, and could not get through either. Yogesh could get through the landline of his house. Seemed like all mobile networks were down. 'Was it due to the rains?' We wondered. On our route from Vasai to Andheri, Yogesh's house came first. He lived on Mira Road. This would be followed by my residence in Borivali and finally, Maqbul would drop Amit off in Andheri before parking the car in the office. Thereafter Maqbul would take a bus to his house in Bandra east. So simple and well chalked out route of 50 kilometres. At least twice every month the four of us, including Maqbul, took this route home. Who knew that nature had fully thwarted our plans that evening?

Till Bhayandar, everything went as usual. We had covered half the distance as any regular day. From there onwards we started experiencing an unusual traffic snarl. From Bhayandar to Mira Road, a three-kilometre distance took us almost two hours. Looking at the stranded traffic, Yogesh decided to get off and walk the rest of the distance. He got down from the car, bid us goodbye, and walked on. Amit and I, along with Maqbul, continued our snail pace journey. By the time we reached Mira Road, we experienced incessant rains and water clogging on the highway. There was traffic all around. Cars, buses, trucks, and vans were stranded. It seemed like many cars were abandoned on the road and there were no occupants inside. At one point, our car could not move any further. We sat in the car waiting and thinking about what to do. From Mira Road onwards, we did not make much progress in our endeavour to reach Borivali and Andheri. Already four hours had passed since we left the bar in Vasai. Water levels on the road were steadily rising. Sitting in our van, we could see that motorbikes and light cars had already started floating. Streets were deserted, with just a handful of people trying to wade through the water. I was only five years in Mumbai, but Amit and Maqbul have spent their whole life in this city. Even they swore that they had never seen such water levels on the highway ever.

I looked at my watch. It was already 11 PM. Did Shreya reach home? I was getting worried for her. I took out my phone, there was zero signal on it. I tried calling her in vain. No calls went through. Neither did I receive any calls from her since we last spoke at 4 PM. Did Yogesh reach home walking through the water? I don't know.

'What should we do?' I asked Amit. He did not answer. Looked like he was equally tense because of the situation.

'Should we walk down through the water?' I spoke again after some time. By the time, the water levels had already covered half of our pretty high car. It would cover half of me if I got out of the car now. I was in double minds.

'It will not be safe to walk down now sir,' replied Maqbul.

'The water levels are high and it's gushing at high speed. The rains also have not stopped. There are chances that we get washed away and hurt ourselves,' he added.

He was right I thought. Moreover, if we fell into an open ditch then we would be dead. We kept on waiting in the car. The water level kept rising with the continuous rain. Dirty water had slowly started creeping in the car. 'The car doors will not be able to resist the gush of water for too long now,' I thought.

At midnight, Amit could not take it anymore.

'I am walking out and trying to reach home,' he said as he tried to push open the right passenger door.

'Don't go, sir, you can't possibly walk through waist-deep water,' Maqbul warned him.

'Amit, we are more than 20 kilometres away from Andheri. How can you walk such a distance in the flood,' I tried to reason with him?

But Amit was adamant to get out. We all were tensed about ourselves and our respective spouses. We were hungry and thirsty too. But Amit had come to the end of his wits. He forced open the door, trying to step out. Flood waters snarled inside the car, even as he tried to step out.

'Amit please do not,' I tried to yell at him, but the sound of rain and gushing waters drowned my voice.

Maqbul and I watched as Amit stepped out and tried to walk past waist-deep waters. He could not. We both saw him fall about ten meters away from our car. I pushed open the left door on my side and tried to get out to help him. Water now rushed in and filled our car. I stepped out but was unable to walk through the strong current. In front of my eyes, I saw Amit fall and get washed away in the flood. He hit a stationery truck as he was carried by the current. Maqbul and I saw him disappear below the truck. By this time Maqbul had also stepped out.

'Sir, sir,' he called out.

'Amit,' I yelled.

Incessant rainfall drowned our voice. We could not see Amit anymore. He got washed away by the current right in front of our gazing eyes. I held the door of the car tightly to save myself from getting washed out too. I did not possess the courage enough to step ahead for ten meters to find Amit. But Maqbul did. He waded across almost his chest-deep water to trace Amit. Since Maqbul had a short built, he found it even more difficult to wade through the water. But he tried. In vain of course. Amit was nowhere to be seen. I became pale with fear and agony as Maqbul came back to the car. We were both standing outside the car, struck with fear. We did not know what to do next. We could barely stand in the water. Our legs were numb. We could not enter the car anymore as water had submerged the inside. I saw my office bag floating on the water.

The water level was still rising, and it would not be safe to be standing on the road. There was water all around us and we lost our ability to think.

'Sir climb on top of the car. Water is rising,' said Maqbul as he stepped on the car window, and swiftly climbed on the roof.

It was not easy for me to climb up. After some struggle and Maqbul's help, I perched myself atop the car. There we sat. Two souls on top of a car as flood water ravaged through the Western Express highway. I did not even look at the time. Every minute looked like an hour. Hungry, thirsty, fully wet, and shivering in fear, we sat there for the rest of the night. Water was everywhere, but we did not have a drop to drink. I tried sobbing relentlessly. I had no clue where Shreya was. I did not have any foresight of what would be happening to us. Maqbul stayed calm and pacified me as much as he could. Even he did not know how his family in the Bandra shanty was faring. We gave each other company and waited through the night for the unknown. No one came to our rescue, no police van, no fire brigade, no Army. The magical city was under water and there was no way anyone could reach us. I could not remember if I had been without food and water for so long ever. Close to dawn, the rain stopped, but precarious clouds still hovered the sky. The flood waters were showing some signs of retreat. But after we had seen what happened to Amit, we did not dare to climb down from the car.

At last, we saw a ray of hope. A rescue team of six men found us perched on the car in the morning. No, these were not government officials, they were locals of Dahisar who had set out on a mission to save stranded people. They were carrying strong ropes and bags of food and water bottles. They approached our car and called out to us. We were still too hesitant to come down. One of the men threw us a rope.

'Tie this around you and you will not get washed away. We are holding the other end tight,' he said.

Maqbul and I tied the rope around our waists and came down from the car. We could barely stand in fatigue. The men opened their bags and offered us bread and water. On that morning the bread tasted no less than Jesus's loaf of bread to us and these men were no less than God.

'Where do you guys stay?' asked one of the men.

'I stay in Borivali and my friend stays in Bandra,' I feebly replied.

'Come with us, we shall walk you to safety. We shall form a human chain, each of us holding on to the rope so that we are not washed off,' said the man.

The six men escorted us for almost five kilometres till we reached Borivali. The walk through the flooded streets took almost two hours. By the time we reached Borivali, the water levels had receded to knee level. One of the men walked further down to Bandra with Maqbul, while the rest bid us goodbye and went ahead on their mission to save more stranded people. I gradually walked towards my house in Raheja Garden, which was only a few meters away.

I came back to the safety of my flat, opened the door, and had no more energy left. I collapsed on the living room sofa. I still had no clue about Shreya. I cannot explain the state that my mind was in. At that moment, the only ask I had from God is to know where Shreya was. I went on trying her number frantically, but it was switched off. I tried calling her office, but no one answered the call. I did not have any of her colleague's numbers. I just could not lie on the sofa anymore. I decided to head out and walk to the Unilever HQ in Andheri, to look for Shreya. I was feeling dead ashamed of myself. How could I drop off into my cosy couch when Shreya was stranded somewhere? I should have gone on her search with those six men. I gathered all my remaining strength and headed towards the main door.

Ding-dong. I heard the bell as I was one foot away from the door. That was probably the sweetest sound I had ever heard. I flung open the door to find Shreya standing there, fully exhausted. I hugged her tight and sobbed my heart out. Shreya too drooped on my shoulders crying relentlessly. First time I saw Shreya break down emotionally. Both of us were equally worried about each other. Shreya had gone back to her office last evening along with her colleague Lata, as they could not traverse beyond Goregaon. They had spent the night in the office and once the water receded in the morning, they started their journey home. The Mumbai floods of 25th July 2005 made us realise how much we loved each other.

'Come on, have your coffee, it's over dear,' said Shreya as we sat down with our coffee and toasts on our balcony.

The skies were still dark with clouds. I was still unable to come out of the trauma of last night. I still did not know how Amit was. Though I tried not to think negatively, the dreadful thought came back to me again and again – was he still alive?

The rains had ceased, and the water almost receded by the next morning. Mumbai was back on its feet. The spirit of Mumbai was undaunted even after the ghastly flood. Within 48 hours the city was back to normal. The streets filled with cars again and the trains with people. The magic of Mumbai was remarkable. Amit was rescued by some people and he was recovering in a hospital in Dahisar. He had a fractured arm and a few bruises and would recover soon. Shreya and I decided to make most of the fallback from the floods. We took a few days off from work and enjoyed our black coffees below the black clouds for the rest of that week. The Mumbai floods of 2005 taught me three valuable lessons for life.

One, Nature is almighty. We should bow to her fury. She is as much a destroyer as a creator.

Two, we should value everyone around us. Life is not a solo journey, and every human we touch becomes a part of our existence. Those six men who came to my rescue in the flood were just ordinary men from the neighbourhood. In a couple of hours when they were steering me to safety, I did not even ask their names. Probably I would never meet them again in life, but they saved my life.

Three, we take relationships so granted. I met Shreya every day at Borivali station when returning from work. We shared a milkshake and walked back home every day. Each evening we took that moment for granted. Nature taught me that all those moments were so valuable. When I was so worried for Shreya that ghastly evening, I realised that every 'tomorrow' may have something unexpected in store for us. So, I decided to make the most of my time with Shreya.

———————

Chapter 5

SINGING IN SINGAPORE

(December 2005)

We were damn excited as we headed towards the immigration counter in the Chhatrapati Shivaji International airport Mumbai. This was our first international trip ever. We wanted to celebrate Christmas in Singapore. We have been dreaming of international vacations, and here we were at the doorstep of our first one. Who knew that this was going to turn into a horrendous vacation which we shall remember all our lives?

Shreya and I were doing well in our marital bond till now. Yes, we did have some tiffs every now and then, but that was quite natural in marital relationships. But honestly, I did have a great time with her. All the other females that I had been with in life till now had completely wiped out from my memory. I was no longer missing the romantic moments with Shreelekha or the sensuous moments with Twinkle. Shreya had combined all of them together. My lifestyle had also changed since my bachelor days. I had moved on from our bachelor boy's accommodation in Kalyan which I used to share with my three other office mates. The 'fantastic four' family, as people in Johnson tiles used to refer to us as, had broken down. Chirag had flown off to a new job in Boston. I left the accommodation as I got married. Shashi and Pradip still occupied the flat in Kalyan. Of course, Shreya and I did visit the infamous flat once after we settled in Mumbai. She was very keen to see how I used to live during my bachelor days.

After marriage, when I brought Shreya to Mumbai, we shifted into a cosy two-bedroom flat in Borivali, in the western suburbs of Mumbai. Shreya had taken all the pain and effort to convert the flat into a proper family household. She had decorated it well, with a proper sofa set and dining table in the living room and two double beds in both the rooms. As icing on the cake, she had also filled the walls with photographs and show pieces. We had a full-fledged family life. My bachelor-day schedules of working late, visiting bars late at night, and sometimes shaking a butt in the infamous Mumbai dance bars had completely transformed. As we reached home from the office around 8 PM, Shreya cooked dinner and I helped her in the kitchen. Post dinner we spent some lovely time together, sometimes going for a stroll, watching a movie, and sometimes on the bed. To be honest, I started liking life after marriage. Quiet in contrast to all the jokes I kept hearing about life after marriage being a bit dreadful.

Of course, we had set some ground rules. I never interfered in Shreya's freedom of shopping and in turn she allowed me my weekend booze. Shreya hailed from a typical Bengali culture where drinking was taboo. Not that I came from a different culture, but with my three years of bachelor life in Mumbai, I had already made it a part of my routine. Shreya was completely ignorant about alcohol and like all Bengali wives was dead against storing and consuming alcohol at home. But I was adamant that I could not have 'dry' weekends. That was our first point of disconnect and marital fight – to booze or not to booze. I eventually convinced her to compromise.

'Shreya, you have two choices,' I said.

'If you don't allow me to drink at home, then I will spend Saturday nights drinking with friends and colleagues in some random bar and you have to spend your weekend evenings alone,' I explained to her.

'On the other hand, if you allow me to drink at home, I can be with you on Saturdays and we might as well drink together. That's way better and cheaper you see,' I tried to logically convince her.

She ultimately relented with two conditions, to which I agreed at once. First, I cannot drink at home when her parents would visit us. Second, I will not force her to drink. Well, I never had to force her to drink. Probably the blue colour shapely bottle of Antiquity whisky was too hard for her to resist. It was one rainy Saturday night when I bought a small

180ml bottle of Antiquity blended whisky and a bottle of soda and came home. I wanted to freshen up first and visited the shower. Post my shower, I was all set for a drink. I got a glass and ice from the kitchen and relaxingly sat on the couch. I picked up the blue bottle from the centre table to pour my first drink. Holy shit. The quarter was fully empty. What the fuck! Did the wine store guy dupe me with an empty bottle? But I was reasonably sure the bottle was full when I left it on the centre table. And I was a regular customer, I was certain that the wine shop guy won't dupe me. I looked at Shreya. I could not believe my ears.

'Nothing much happened even after I gulped the whole bottle,' she said.

'People say whisky makes one tipsy, but I did not feel a thing,' she added.

She had finished 180ml of whisky, neat. Wow! Now I don't have to look elsewhere for a drinking partner. Thereafter, whisky became the third and regular partner of our fun-filled Saturday evenings.

'How could you be so careless?' I was utterly shocked and equally upset with Shreya's carelessness.

'Why are you blaming me? How will I guess that the purse can get stolen from under our noses? You should have been more vigilant.' She answered back.

'What do you mean Shreya. Don't pass the blame on me. Am I supposed to take care of your purse?' I shouted back. The whole restaurant looked at us.

I did not know what to do next. It felt as if the sky had fallen on my head. How do we get back home now?

Up till this juncture, we have been enjoying our first overseas vacay in sensational Singapore. We had a great flight. It was also the first time that I could ask for free beers on a flight. Though the Singapore Airlines air hostess was a bit hostile when I asked for the fourth beer, nonetheless I did drench myself with beers through the five hours flight. The only discomfort I was facing was to be without a smoke for five hours. I don't remember being so long without a fag, ever since I started smoking during the second year of my college. We landed in Singapore early in the morning. The first thing I visited was the airport smoking room. Then when we passed immigration and came out of the airport, I was so excited to have a lavish cab ride in a Toyota Corolla. In Mumbai, we had the mundane black and yellow fiats as taxis. Here in Singapore most of the cabs were different versions of Toyota. I had only seen such cars in movies till then.

Through our next four days of vacation, we hopped around the city. We saw Sentosa Island, where we saw the Aquarium and the Singapore Lion. We loved the ropeway ride to the island. We also loved the Singapore night safari. We freaked out eating seafood in Clark Quay and walked up and down on Orchard Road. We got mesmerized by the MRT underground transport. It was so much better than the only underground metro that we had in India. We had never seen such clean public transport ever. We were having the time of our lives. We were mentally and physically away from work. Shreya's and my respective desks at Kodak and Coca-Cola had been left empty for a whole week now. But all good things come to an end. We finally reached the last evening of our first international vacation. We were scheduled to fly back to Mumbai the next day. All was going well, until our last dinner in Singapore.

We came for dinner in an uptown Asian Restaurant on Orchard Road. It supposedly served the best Asian food in all of Asia. It was quite a large place with inside and outdoor seating arrangements. We chose to sit outside. The outside area was dimly lit and offered a good romantic environment for our closing dinner in Singapore. Shreya and I were sitting and chatting, while she slung her purse on the rim of her chair. After dinner, when we were getting up to leave, she suddenly realised her purse was missing. I completely lost my cool. Not that her purse had too many dollars, most of the money was in my purse. But her purse had her passport. I did not know what to do. How would we take our flight back the next day? I yelled at Shreya for her carelessness. The whole restaurant was looking at us.

Usually, in such moments, I tended to lose my cool. I am a person who cannot stay composed in moments of crisis. How do we go back to India? Should we go to the Police? Even if the Police help us finding the stolen purse, how would we pay for the extended stay in the Hotel? All negative thoughts crippled me in such moments of crisis. Shreya was just the opposite. She became calmer during such situations. That irritated me even more. The same was the situation at the restaurant. While I came to the end of my wits, Shreya put on her thinking cap to find a solution to the mess that we had landed into. As a first step, she started questioning the restaurant waiters and the guests on the other tables, if they noticed anyone picking up her purse. They did not. Then she enquired with the Hotel Manager if they had any CCTV installed. They did but that was only in the enclosed part of the restaurant. Unfortunately, we chose to dine in the open-air area of the joint and this part did not have any cameras. So, after all her efforts, we were back to square one. Shreya was without her passport and I without my wits on what we should do next. Shreya asked the manager about the nearest police post and then we came out of the restaurant.

I had, by this time, lost all hope and left it to Shreya to find a solution.

'What do we do now, Shreya?' I asked.

'As a first step, we report the loss to the Police. Then, tomorrow morning you get in touch with your office in Singapore and ask for help. As a third step, we ask the hotel to extend our booking for another three days,' she said calmly.

'I don't know anyone in Coca-Cola Singapore. Even if I did, how will that help,' I said?

'Let us hope that they have some contacts with the Indian Embassy,' said Shreya.

What a vacation, I thought. That's what happens if we step out of the country. Had this happened in any Indian state, we would have just lost a few bucks, that's it. Here, we are stranded without a passport. I shall never leave my country again, I thought. I was almost in tears, while Shreya led the entire conversation at the Police Post. The officer was cooperative. He took down all our details – names, address in Singapore, address in India, my passport number, etc. We returned to the Hotel close to 11 PM. Shreya went to the reception, explained our situation, and asked for an extension for a three-night stay. The receptionist happily extended our booking. She also advised us to get in touch with the Indian Embassy the next morning. She also gave us the address of the Coca-Cola Singapore office, at Shreya's request. That night, I could not sleep. I just did not see a way to get out of the shit that Shreya's carelessness had put us into. On the other side of the bed, the lady who lost her passport was sleeping soundly.

The next morning, we went to the Coca-Cola office. I explained my situation at the reception while disclosing my identity of being a Manager with Coca-Cola India. The receptionist listened to me attentively and directed me to the local HR department. Cynthia, from the personnel department, met us in some time and took us to a conference room. I shall never forget how Cynthia helped us. She had given us a contact to meet in the Indian Embassy and even arranged a free stay for us at the company guest house in the Singapore Harbour Front. I also, in my mind, thanked Shreya for coming up with the idea of contacting the Coca-Cola office. Thereafter the process was long but smooth. We contacted Devendra Saini at the Indian Embassy. Cynthia had already spoken to him and briefed him of the help that we needed. I thanked my lucky stars for possessing a copy of our passport and visas. I don't know how, but something inside me had asked me to take a photocopy of the visa, tickets, and passport when we planned our trip last month. Luckily, I carried these copies along and that made the job at the Embassy much smoother. They could dig out all our info about the travel into Singapore. We had to apply for an 'Emergency Certificate' citing that our passport was lost, and we had to return to India urgently. Devendra helped us right through the process and within the next four days we were all set to return to India with Shreya's Emergency Certificate. Ultimately, though we went through a lot of tense moments, we did have an extended vacation in Singapore.

I was so happy to land in Mumbai once again. All's well that ends well. I learned three lessons from the incident.

First, it is so important to keep cool in a crisis and think of solutions rather than dwelling on the problem.

Second, I am so lucky to have such a calm lady beside me and I shall depend on her in all my crises.

Third, though I dread going for another vacation abroad, if we at all do, I am going to be carrying both our passports for safe custody.

———

Chapter 6

In the Wrong Place

(July 2008)

Shreya and I had never heard of the term ectopic pregnancy until we googled. We were getting more and more tensed as the beta HCG count had crossed the 25000 mark and yet Dr Shweta Nalawade could not find the foetus in Shreya's uterus. Google told us that at such beta count the foetus is usually prominently visible through sonography, and if it is not, chances are that the pregnancy was ectopic. It had been seven weeks since Shreya had tested pregnant and we had kept the news secret even from our own family members. I finally decided that we should speak to my own sister, who was a gynaecologist herself. Neither of our phones had an ISD facility, so I visited an STD/ISD booth nearby. It has been several months since I last visited an STD/ISD booth. I used to use such booths to call Shreya from Mumbai before our marriage. This time I was here to call Aarushi in Vancouver. It was a Sunday evening, around 7 PM, which meant it was around 9.30 AM on a Sunday morning for Aarushi. I felt this was the time that would have the highest probability to find Aarushi at home. I was right. She answered the call after five rings.

'Good morning, Dr Aarushi here,' she answered the call formally.

'Didi, this is Abhinav,' I answered from my end.

She was utterly surprised to find a call from me. I usually did not call her very often. Though we were very close in our childhood days, times had changed. We lived in different corners of the world and were busy in our own personal worlds. She was married and had two children to manage. I was married and at this moment struggling with my pregnant wife. I told her all about Shreya's pregnancy and our doubts about it being ectopic. She was utterly concerned about hearing my story, both as a doctor and as a sister. Her concern reassured me that even though our phone calls had died down, our bond as siblings had not.

'You are saying that the beta count is 25000 and the baby is not visible?' She asked to re-confirm.

'Yes, Didi.'

'In that case, there are 100% chances that it is an ectopic pregnancy. Your doctor did not suspect it?' She asked.

'No, Dr Nalawade did not tell us this term, we googled it and called you.'

'Did she do an internal sonography?' She asked.

'No. She told us internal sonography may harm the foetus.'

'If that's what she said, then change your doctor immediately. Go and visit another gynaecologist and ask the doctor to negate ectopic.' She instructed.

'What is an ectopic pregnancy, Didi?'

'It's a pregnancy when the foetus is formed in the fallopian tube and not in the uterus. The ovulation has happened in the wrong place. The situation can be dangerous if not acted upon right away,' now the doctor in her was speaking.

'Does it mean, the baby will not be born?'

'If it is in the fallopian tube, then definitely not. The tube cannot create space for the foetus to grow. If the foetus is not immediately aborted, it may cause the tube to burst and that can be fatal for Shreya.'

I was shocked and speechless for a moment.

Aarushi continued, 'Don't get disheartened, take Shreya to another doctor immediately. It is more important to save her than an unborn foetus. Take her to a doctor today.'

'Didi, today is Sunday, and it's already past seven in the evening in Mumbai. We will not find a doctor now. Can I take her tomorrow morning?' I asked feebly.

'Absolutely not. With a beta count of 25000, you cannot take the risk at all. Take her to the emergency ward of a good hospital. I am sure doctors shall be available there,' she said.

'OK, will do,' I said, almost in tears now.

'Keep me posted. You can text me and I shall call you back. All the best,' Aarushi hung up.

The world as if fell on me as I walked back home. I could see our dreams come crashing down. How do I share the conversation with Shreya? I had never felt so low before in life, not even when Shreelekha had dumped me. But I need to muster the courage. Which was the nearest hospital to our house? Fortis, Kandivali I thought. The date was 21st July and it was Shreya's birthday. We both were tense because of our situation, and the date had almost slipped my mind. I did buy a gift for Shreya though. Yesterday I had bought a large teddy bear soft toy from the local Archies Gallery. But, with the proceedings of my call with Aarushi, it was probably the most inappropriate gift to give her now. Instead, I had to explain the situation of emergency to her. What a wrong day and wrong place to celebrate a birthday. I had no choice. It was more important to save Shreya than to celebrate her birthday. She was eagerly waiting at home to hear what Aarushi has said. How I wished, I had better news to share.

In the next one hour, we were seated in the emergency ward of Fortis Hospital, waiting for Dr Kishori Kadam to check Shreya. The doctor had to either negate or confirm an ectopic pregnancy. Both of us were almost shattered. I was still praying against hope and trying to convince Shreya that probably it was not ectopic. Probably the baby would show up in the sonography today. I was right, the baby did show itself on the sonography today, unfortunately in the wrong place. The foetus had formed inside the left fallopian tube.

'See this, it is in the wrong place,' said Dr Kadam, pointing to the blurry image of the foetus on the screen.

The first image of the baby is probably what every woman craves to see. This gives eternal joy to every woman. For Shreya, it turned out to be the most dreadful moment of her life. The foetus was clearly visible on her swelled left fallopian tube. Shreya burst out in tears.

'How come we could not see the baby in Dr Nalawade's clinic?' I asked Dr Kadam.

'It was probably the make and quality of the machine she was using. An advanced machine could have detected the ectopic much earlier and the situation would not be as worse,' replied Dr Kadam.

I was speechless. But, true to her nature, Shreya had composed herself from her initial shock. She had already come to terms with the situation. She had understood that this was a failed pregnancy. She wore her logical corporate manager cap and started understanding the next steps from the doctor.

'If you had approached me earlier, the foetus could have been ejected without an operation,' explained Dr Kadam.

'How would you have ejected the foetus?' Asked Shreya.

'We use a drug called methotrexate to kill the foetus and then the foetus gradually dissolves without harming the tube. But now we cannot take the risk. It is already too big to try out that route now,' said the doctor.

'What are the next steps?' Shreya asked in her corporate tone.

'We have to operate immediately. If I can get one of the three operation theatres free, we shall do it tonight itself,' said Doctor Kadam.

'What kind of operation doctor?' asked Shreya.

I was amazed at the composure Shreya demonstrated. How could she manage to be so calm when her dreams were shattered thirty minutes ago?

The doctor explained the procedure to both of us. Shreya would undergo laparoscopic surgery. An incision would be made and the entire left fallopian tube, along with the foetus would be cut off and extracted.

'Get her admitted right away,' added Dr Kadam, looking at me.

I had completely broken down. But Shreya was thankfully steady, though I could feel what must be going on inside her. While Shreya was wheeled away to the ICU, I completed the hospital admission formalities. Without Shreya by my side, I just could not bear the pain of losing a child who was still unborn. I felt lonely, sad, and totally shattered.

Ring, Ring, Ring…… my cell phone rang. Shashi's name was being displayed on the screen. Should I pick it? I thought. I badly wanted to share my feelings with my best pal, but would he understand. Finally, I picked up on the seventh ring.

'What's up Abhi, how many pegs down on a Sunday evening?' Shashi said cheerfully, of course completely unaware of my situation.

'I am in the Fortis Kandivali, Shashi, can we talk later,' I said as composed as possible. Though I badly wanted to share my depression, I decided not to trouble him on a Sunday evening.

But Shashi was of different mettle. He did not let me just hang up the call. I had to finally give in and narrate the whole incident and tell him what I was doing in Fortis.

'Fucker, you are telling me all this now. Could you not have called me at least when you came to Fortis?' said Shashi, seeming quite upset.

'I will manage Shashi, don't spoil your and Shalini's evening?' I said, still acting to be composed. Shalini and Shashi had got married last year and were still enjoying their double income no kid days. I did not feel like disturbing their weekend.

'Shut up and cut the call. We will be there in the next hour. Keep calm,' he said and hung up.

I completed the admission formalities and went up to the ICU. I could see Shreya on the other side of the ICU door. The security outside the ICU did not let me in. I waited outside the door desperately wanting to know whether Shreya was going to be operated on. I did not have to wait too long. Soon, Dr Kadam came out and informed me that the OT was ready, and Shreya would be operated on within the next hour. I saw Shreya being wheeled out of the ICU. She smiled at me as she passed by. I tried to smile back but couldn't. I followed her through the corridor, to the entrance of the OT. This is where we had to part. I could feel my eyes moisten once again. I never felt so alone and helpless. The OT door shut on me, with

Shreya on the other side. I closed my eyes and could not hold back my tears.

I could feel a soft hand around my shoulder. I opened my eyes and found Shalini holding me and Shashi standing by my side. I never realised when they had come and stood beside me. Yes, I felt very light on seeing them. A grief shared is really grief halved, I could sense the meaning of the saying now. I broke down on Shalini's shoulder. She held me tight without saying a word.

Shashi, Shalini, and I stood still outside the operation theatre for the next one hour. None of us spoke a word. I really did not know what to say. By that time, I had come to terms with the fact that I was not going to be a father. I was just praying that Shreya come out safely through the OT door once again and we go home together.

Shashi broke the silence first

'Did you think of names for the child when you have one?' he asked with a smile.

'Is this the time for such tomfoolery you fucker. Shreya is having a laparoscopy inside and not a caesarean,' I screamed at him.

'I know that full well nut head. I said WHEN you have a child what would you name him or her?' he said still smiling.

'Surely, this is not the last time you guys are going to try, right?' Shashi added.

Somehow, I felt nice hearing what Shashi just said. He was right. That is probably the best answer to Shreya and my grief. Why not try again? I saw a ray of hope. That's the first thing I shall tell Shreya as she comes out. I thought. Thanks, Shashi, for making me see the brighter side of things, I thought and smiled. Probably I genuinely smiled the first time that evening. Friends in need were friends indeed. In my mind, I thanked Shashi and Shalini for being by my side today. Probably, I was too weak to face this pain alone. Only a few hours ago Shreya and I were weaving dreams of having a baby and now I am just waiting eagerly for the baby to be removed from its wrong place. In another forty-five minutes, the operation was done. Doctor Kadam walked out of the OT with a pleasant smile on her face.

'All done. Shreya is fine now. I have taken out the left fallopian tube along with the foetus' she said as she walked to me.

'Can I take her home now madam?' I asked a stupid question

'No. She will be under ICU observation for a day, you can take her home tomorrow evening,' the doctor smiled again as she walked away.

In another fifteen minutes, Shreya was wheeled back to her bed in ICU. She was still unconscious. The nurse told me that she would take another hour to get out of her anaesthesia effect. I waited patiently outside the ICU along with Shashi and Shalini. After about an hour we got permission to see Shreya. Although she had regained consciousness, she was still in a stupor from the effects of the anaesthesia. She smiled at me and then looked at Shashi and Shalini.

'How are you,' I asked taking her hands in mine.

'I saw the foetus,' she replied. 'It looked like a lump of flesh,' she said with a drop of tear trickling down her eyes.

'Hey, we shall surely see a baby within a year, you can think of names as you rest,' I said, trying to look jovial.

'Don't worry, I am fine. Only a bit of pain down the stomach,' replied Shreya with a smile.

'You rest dear, you shall be fine tomorrow and we shall go home,' I tried to encourage her.

I released her hand and slowly left the ICU allowing her to rest.

'Have you eaten anything the whole evening?' asked Shashi as we came out into the hospital corridor.

I shook my head. I never thought of food since the time we came to Fortis. I did not feel hunger or thirst at all. Grief can take over one's physical needs, I guess.

'We haven't had dinner either; care for a beer?' grinned Shashi.

'What? Shashi is this the way to behave in a hospital?' Shalini snarled at Shashi.

'You don't know my friend, but I do. Beer is the only thing that can cheer him up,' Shashi said, unshaken at Shalini's snarl.

'Come one,' Shashi pulled me by my hand, 'let's celebrate Shreya's successful and safe operation. At least the sword swaying over Shreya has been destroyed.'

Shalini stayed back at the hospital, in case, Shreya needed something. Shashi and I headed to a nearby bar for a drink and some grub. Shashi promised to bring back a packed sandwich for Shalini on our way back. I relished the beer, it soothed down my tensed nerves. At last, I felt back in my senses as I sipped on the chilled Kingfisher.

'Why did it happen to us Shashi? Only two percent of pregnancy cases turn ectopic. Then why us out of all people? Why did God do this to us?' I said in a mild stupor from the beer.

'You know what Abhi, God gives just as much sorrow to you that you can bear. Probably only two percent of people can bear the pain of ectopic pregnancy and you are the chosen one,' he said.

'He was probably right. It would be much more painful to lose a born child than an unborn one,' I reflected. Both of us fell silent for some time.

'What name would rhyme with Abhinav?' Shashi asked with his classic grin.

'How would Abhijeet sound for a son and Abhilasha for a daughter,' he said looking at me through the corner of his eyes.

'There you go again fucker,' I smiled as I picked up my beer glass.

'Here's to your next attempt pal, cheers,' Shashi picked up his glass and clinked against mine.

The next evening Shreya was discharged from Fortis. We were sitting across Dr Kadam in her chamber as she was signing the discharge certificate.

'What would be my chances to get pregnant again,' Shreya asked the doctor. I was happy to see Shreya back in her corporate logical thinking image. 'That's much better than being emotional about the loss,' I thought.

'Now that you have just one tube left the chances of a normal pregnancy would be 50%. I would advise not to try naturally conceiving again as the result may be ectopic again. Usually, once a person is prone to ectopic the same may repeat,' explained Doctor Kadam.

'Why does one become ectopic? Any particular reason?' asked Shreya.

'It's very difficult to pinpoint on any particular reason. It is to do with the size and alignment of the tubes which can't be changed. But once you have an ectopic, you should be careful. After intercourse, if you miss your periods, you should immediately get a beta test done and if it is positive, please contact me immediately,' said Doctor Kadam.

'If naturally conceiving is not advisable, then what other methods should we try doctor?' I asked a logical question this time.

'We can try IVF, In Vitro Fertilization. It's an expensive process but can give safe and sure results,' she said.

'When can we try that?' I asked quickly

'Let her get fully fit first. See me for a repeat check-up after a month and then we can talk more about the process,' said the doctor with a smile.

We thanked the doctor and came out of the hospital. Shashi drove us back home. Shreya and I were sitting in the rear seat. She was leaning on my shoulder.

None of us spoke a word through the twenty minutes of the journey. I pondered, in silence, over the three lessons I had learned over the last 24 hours at the Fortis hospital.

One, it really pains when dreams get shattered. I could not remember any other incident in life that was more painful to me than losing an unborn foetus. I did not feel as devastated even on the day I lost my dad.

Two, humans live on hope, and hope is the best healer to help us move on. I remembered Shashi's words. Abhijeet would be my child's name if he was a boy and Abhilasha if she was a girl. The hope that we can get back to Fortis again with Shreya pregnant in the right way, would help us move on in life.

Third, friends like Shashi and Shalini, who stood beside us in the time of utter crisis is a gift of God. I will be indebted to them for the rest of my existence.

Chapter 7

TRYING THE TEST TUBE TOUR

(November 2008)

'Come on fast, you can't have the room the whole day,' said the nurse from outside while knocking on the closed door.

There I sat inside the dimly lit room, fully naked, holding my penis in my right hand and a glass container on the other. Moments ago, the fat, dark and ugly nurse had given this container to me and shoved me inside this room expecting me to be out in one minute with my sperms collected inside the sanitized container. What the fuck! This was not as easy as collecting urine for a urine test. Getting a sperm test done was more complicated than I imagined.

Shreya and I were back with doctor Kishori Kadam almost after five months from the time we last met her. We finally decided to try a baby through the IVF route, which was commonly known as getting a test tube baby.

It took Shreya some time to recover from the initial shock of ectopic pregnancy, both mentally and physically. Though I could share her mental pain of an abortion, the physical element of going through surgery was borne by her alone. It took more than six weeks for her to be able to lead a normal life again. The next few months we tried to forget the incident by concentrating on our respective careers once again. Within three years of joining Unilever, Shreya had bagged a promotion. I too got busy owing to the festive season. For a cold drink business, the Indian regional festive months of September, October, and November are very crucial, and work really triples up. September brings Ganapati to Mumbai; October follows with Navratri while November calls for Diwali sales. So, for a few months, we were drowned in work and hardly conversed on the next course of action about having a child in life. It was when we took a short vacation after Diwali that our minds once again started thinking about having a child.

'Should we do an IVF when we go back,' asked Shreya while sipping on her coffee.

We were holidaying in Bali, Indonesia at that time.

'Is this the time to talk about IVF, Shreya,' I asked?

'Why can't we just enjoy the beach?' I added.

'I really want to have a child now. Let's try it, please,' pleaded Shreya.

Since she had an ectopic pregnancy, we were very clear that we are not going to try having a baby through the natural route anymore. From that time, I ensured to have protected intercourse, lest she becomes pregnant again. IVF was the only route. I researched on it quite a lot during the past few months, without letting Shreya know. IVF was the 'unnatural' way of having a baby without having sex. Sperm is taken from the male and an ovule from the female and the mating is done inside the laboratory. And bingo, an egg is formed outside the womb. 'What a technology!' I wondered. Then the egg is injected directly inside the uterus of the mother, where the baby starts forming. Whether the egg will convert into a baby was of course a matter of chance. IVF technology in no way guaranteed a child, but it did ensure that an ectopic pregnancy is avoided completely. That's exactly why I got hooked on IVF instead of the natural route. Of course, the procedure was damn expensive. With god's grace, we had a joint bank account healthy enough to support IVF costs. I was just dilly-dallying to give Shreya the time to get back to her comfort zone. Now that she had raised the topic; I was super excited.

'Ok, let's meet Doctor Kadam as the first thing after we get back to Mumbai,' I answered with a smile.

And that's how I landed up in the dimly lit room holding my penis in my right hand.

Though I had researched well on the advantages and costs of an IVF, I did not detail enough on the procedure. Doctor Kadam explained this to us in detail. It started with doing a battery of blood tests, followed by a sperm test. And for the sperm test, of course, I had to give her a sample of my sperm. And that's exactly why the fatso nurse pushed me inside this room with a container, expecting me to bring it back filled with my ejaculation. Easier said than done. Forget ejaculating, my friend Mr Penis refused to even stand up to the occasion. Although there were a host of erotic magazines lined up on a table in the room to help my organ to rise and fulfill the task, somehow these naked damsel pictures were not helping me much. The picture that came back repeatedly in front of my eyes was of the old, fat ugly nurse who was constantly knocking on the door pestering me to hurry up. What performance pressure! At last, with a hell of a lot of sweat, I managed to get a meagre drop out from my friend who was tightly stroked by my right hand. Voila, I came out victorious with a drop of white liquid inside the container. I proudly handed over my laurel to the nurse and left for the day. I never imagined that a sperm test would be more difficult than my PG exams. And guess what, on the day of the results, I did come to know that the sperm test was indeed more difficult. I did pass my PG exams with flying colours but miserably failed the sperm test.

'The good news is that all the blood tests are fine, you are an absolute fit couple,' said Doctor Kadam, glancing through the array of test reports perched on her table.

'But I do have bad news too.' She continued.

Both of us looked at each other in despair and then eagerly looked at the doctor.

'What is it, doctor?' Shreya asked.

'Abhinav, your sperm count is not adequate to have an IVF,' came the precise and blunt reply from the doctor.

I was stunned. What is she saying? My sperm count was low? And I did not know it all these years? Was this possible? Hands-on my heart, I have slept with four women in my life till now – Shreelekha my first girlfriend, Twinkle my second, Maria a professional sex mate, and of course Shreya (My feats about this can be found in my book 'Lollypops to Cigarettes). I am reasonably sure that in each case I had done a good job in ejaculating inside them, at least none of them complained. And today I am told by a professional sperm tester that my white substance was not good enough to be a father. Shreya as usual remained calmed and composed to the news.

'Is there any medication to improve sperm count,' she asked.

'Well, there is none too effective, one has to control lifestyle, eat healthy, exercise, avoid smoking and drinking, and the sperm count may improve,' replied the doc.

'What would be the time frame for such improvement?' Shreya was again wearing the corporate questions hat.

'Well, that depends. But there is another way out to continue the IVF procedure,' replied Dr Kadam.

'And that is?' I pitched in this time.

'Well, we can go for a sperm donor. Meaning the ovules will be from Shreya and the sperms from someone else, who has a better count.'

I felt humiliated and infuriated at the same time. The doctor was virtually suggesting that Shreya carries someone else's child in her womb. I shall never let that happen for sure, even if it means going childless for the rest of our lives. I had to do something.

'Can I get another chance doctor,' I pleaded?

'To be honest, that day in the donation room, I felt out of place that I could not ejaculate well. Probably that was the cause why the sperm count was low,' I went on to explain.

This explanation did get the doctor thinking a bit.

'Well,' she said after a brief pause, 'We can do that, we can get you tested once again,'

I saw a ray of hope. I was doubly sure that if I had to go into the same room and try again, I shall fail again.

'Well, doctor, can I take the container home and fill it at home? I shall bring it back when done' I said.

I felt that if I could ejaculate in the comfort of my own bathroom, I would do a much better job in giving the right sample with enough sperms in it. I have, just as any other man, done multiple ejaculations in the comfort of my own bathroom. I continued to stare at Dr Kadam, hoping to get her permission to do the sperm sample collection at home.

'Where do you stay?' asked the doctor.

'I stay in Borivali East, Madam,' I answered, though I was a bit surprised by the question. What had my address got to do with my sperm count?

Probably the doc guessed the question from my face.

'The life of sperm in normal temperature is not more than half an hour. After ejaculation, we need to keep the sperms under laboratory conditions', she explained.

Now I was clear why she was asking for my whereabouts. The Raheja Gardens, where we stayed was hardly a fifteen minutes driving distance from the hospital if one drove in the early hours of the morning. In my mind, I planned it already. I would collect the sperm at home and then drive down to the hospital and hand it over to the fat nurse. It would be much more comforting than sitting in that dark room stroking my penis for futile results.

The next morning, I was being driven at full speed by Shashi to the hospital, as I sat on the passenger seat with the container full of my sperms held tightly between my palms. Ultimately Dr Kadam gave me the second chance and relented to my idea of collecting the sperms in my own bathroom. I shared my plans with Shashi, and he was eager to help, as always. We had to make sure that we make the journey to the hospital from my house in no more than twenty minutes. So, I entrusted the driving to Shashi, who was by far the best driver I knew. He was ready at 7.30 AM outside my apartment, sitting in the car with the ignition on. I was working out with my organ, to the best of my ability in my bathroom. I did not want to fail again and wanted to gift Dr Kadam the best of my sperms. As I stood below the shower with my penis in my right hand, I wondered which fantasy would help me get aroused and perform well. Ultimately what came to my mind was the first shower I ever had with a lady with me. Twinkle, it was. In my second year of college when I had gone to an overnight picnic with my classmates, I had a shower followed by sex with my classmate Twinkle (reference taken from my book Lollypops to Cigarettes). That scene in the shower with Twinkle came back to me as I stood below ejaculating. Within seconds the container was half full.

'We did it in exactly 19 minutes,' I told Shashi, giving him a high five.

The container was in safe custody and I was hopeful that I pass the sperm test this time. Within 24 hours the result was out. I passed with flying colours and now I did not need the support of another man to become a father. I was far from imagining then, that I would need the support of a woman other than Shreya to gift me, my first child.

The IVF procedure started soon. It was not a fun procedure for sure, especially for Shreya. As a first step, ovules were drawn out of Shreya and scientifically copulate with my sperms. This resulted in the formation of eight eggs in the doctor's laboratory. Then three of the eight eggs were carefully injected inside Shreya's uterus and left to grow into a foetus. But even then, a baby was not a guarantee. It may or may not form, the chances were fifty-fifty, as per the doctor. This was followed by daily injections put on Shreya, consecutively for 30 days to boost the egg. It was a painful time for her. Every evening, after coming back from the office, Shreya and I reported to Doctor Kadam's clinic to be injected with a booster. If all this would have yielded results, we would have forgotten the pain. But alas, even IVF could not make us parents, and we were back to square one, sitting with the doctor in her chambers. A lot of energy, time, and money went down the drain.

'Unfortunately, Shreya, the baby was not formed. But we can try again,' said the doctor calmly.

'And we shall have to repeat the whole process and pay two lacs of rupees again?' Shreya said, visibly upset with the results.

'Don't get disheartened, IVFs sometimes fail in the first attempt. Since five more eggs are already stored with us, the second process is simpler and cheaper,' explained the doctor.

'When do we start again?' asked Shreya.

'Well, you can take a month of rest. After that we shall inject three eggs in your uterus once again and hope for the best,' smiled the doctor.

I was in no mood to try the whole damn thing again. I did not want to see Shreya go through mental and physical torture once again. I was happy the way we were. We don't have a baby, so what? Our peers and friends around had little kids to play with. Great, God does not give everything to everyone, right? We need to learn to live life the way it is, I tried to justify with Shreya. But she was headstrong to give it another shot. So, our repeat telecast of the whole event continued. Once again eggs were injected into Shreya. Once again, we made thirty trips to the clinic to get Shreya injected with boosters. The only thing we did differently was to visit the local Sai Baba temple every day while returning from the clinic. Since nature and science failed to give us a baby, we resorted to divine powers. We prayed hard every day to see a baby soon. Probably Baba had a bit of misunderstanding, he did send a baby after all but to Shalini and Shashi. Please don't be mistaken, we were relentlessly happy with their success and not at all envious. It's just that we felt a tinge of pain in our hearts when we saw that our mission to become parents was far from being materialised.

The results of the second IVF were the same as the first. The doctor did cut a sorry face. But she accepted the cheque worth one lac rupees any which way. We were back to square one with some amounts of money drawn out from our joint bank savings. I was done with it. I blamed my fate and was ready to move on in life. But my Shreya, my strong and bold Shreya was sinking into depression in front of my eyes. She talked and ate very little. She started losing weight She stopped attending social gatherings and began spending long hours at work. I tried to pacify her as much as I could but speaking about the whole incident upset her even more. So, we both stopped speaking about it. Friends and family kept on bothering us on our plans to start a family, and we found all possible innovative ways to duck the question. Being a father was not my fate probably.

I walked back to the Sai Baba temple one day, this time alone. It was past noon and the temple was relatively empty. Good for me, I wanted to have a monologue with the Baba. Locals here believed that Sai Baba works miracles for devotees who visit this temple, unfortunately, Shreya and I did not get the proof of the pudding.

'Why did you do this to us, Baba?' I asked.

'What do you want my child?' a voice within me said.

'All I want is Shreya to be happy, I just don't want to see her depressed,' I answered.

'Close your eyes and visualise in your mind, and you shall see what I want to show you,' said the voice in my subconscious.

I followed the instruction. With closed eyes, I visualised Shreya and me getting down from a large black sedan outside the temple. We had a baby in our arms. We enter the temple as the chauffeur took the car away. We walked up the steps and stood in front of the Baba with folded arms. The baby looked at the Baba and smiled.

My imagination bought a smile to my face. 'Come on,' I said to myself. Now don't start believing in miracles. 'Everything I saw was a part of my subconscious,' I thought and smiled at my own foolery. 'Miracles like this happened only in films,' I thought, as I started walking away from the temple. I did not believe in daydreams at all. The bell of the temple rang at that very moment. Probably, I should have believed in Sai Baba that day.

———————

Chapter 8

MIRACLES DO OCCUR

(June 2013)

'Dada…dada…dada,' little Abhijeet toddled towards me as I entered the house.

I have been dying to hear this voice from my little son. I have been missing this voice over the last two weeks since I had gone on a business training to New York. This voice, this call from my son washed away my sixteen hours of jet lag as soon as I entered home. This was the first outstation trip I made since Abhijeet was born. These fourteen days made me realise the actual bonding between a father and a son. I profusely thanked Sulekha for bearing the child for Shreya and me, that too at a point in life when we had almost given up the hope of being parents.

Many a time I have debated in my own mind if those two years after our IVF failures were good or bad for our future. Those two years were the most depressing time for our family life while the most successful years of our career. Shreya and I were devastated after her ectopic pregnancy and thereafter two subsequent failed IVF attempts. We lost all hopes to become parents even though we deeply wanted to be. The social stigma was an added wound to the bruise. Both of us were passing through a rough phase of depression. Even our close family felt that we had prioritised our careers over parenthood. Had we not delayed the issue of having a child for five years since our marriage we would not have landed in soup, our respective families felt. To overcome the depression, Shreya and I decided to avoid as many social gatherings as possible and concentrate on our careers. If people felt we were career-oriented, so be it. Let us excel there at least.

Shreya and I came even closer to each other during this phase. The ectopic pregnancy was a curse of nature and we could not do anything about it. The failure of two IVF attempts was also not in our hands. Only we could understand the pain that we were going through. All our friends and companions had a baby, somehow God had left that desire unfulfilled for us. At this point, we decided to make our respective work and career become our only solace to our failure to be parents. Shreya quickly jumped up the corporate ladder during these two years through her sheer dedication and hard work. Unilever reciprocated by rewarding her with two subsequent promotions. From Manager to Senior Manager and GM Supply chain thereafter. Not a mean feat for her for sure. Not many employees in Unilever could brag of two levels of escalation in such a short period. I too did not want to be left behind. I changed ship – from Coca-

Cola to PepsiCo. I joined PepsiCo Mumbai as the Regional Logistics Manager for their West zone. Not many species could boast of testing waters in both the beverage giants. I soon became quite popular in PepsiCo for this feat of mine.

Work-life became smooth and we were carrying more to the bank as a DINK couple than ever before. We also happily spent a bit of the dough on ourselves. While envious eyes looked on, we changed our Maruti Alto to a new black Toyota Corolla. We had three vacations during these two years. The first was in the USA. We spent our sixth anniversary eve in a chopper over Las Vegas city, an experience that many of our age could not even imagine. The second was in the city of love Paris where we sipped champagne from the same glass on the top of the Eiffel Tower. We felt as if we relived our days of sharing a banana shake at the Borivali station. The third vacation was amongst the serene beauty of the Indian Ocean in the Maldives. It was in the Maldives that we met Sulekha and our lives changed forever. Right till our last breath we shall be thanking our lucky stars that we holidayed in the Maldives and had a chance encounter with Sulekha and her husband Promod. This is where I started to believe in miracles. This is probably how Sai Baba planned our destiny. We lost our foetus to an ectopic pregnancy and that's how our desire to become parents became much stronger. We then failed on IVF and our desire became even more deeply rooted. It was probably Sai Baba's design that we happened to holiday in the Maldives at the same time as Sulekha and Promod and that we were destined to ride on the same boat that morning.

While in the Maldives, we decided to go for a trip inside the ocean to watch dolphins. The resort that we were staying in organized dolphin-watching trips every morning. On the trip, the tourists are taken on a boat inside the ocean where dolphins feed every morning. On the third day of our vacation, Shreya and I booked a dolphin watch trip with the reception. The next morning, we were escorted from our room to a jetty. A small speed boat was waiting at the jetty to take us into the sea and see the dolphins.

'The boat ride would take about half an hour, then we park at sea for about an hour where we can see the dolphins. If you want more adventure, you can also snorkel in the sea while the boat is parked. Thereafter we return to the hotel' said the hotel guide explaining the whole trip to us.

Shreya and I were super excited and all set to set foot on the boat.

'We shall have to wait for five more minutes Sir, there is one more couple who shall be joining us on the same boat,' said the driver of the boat.

Our spirits dampened a bit on hearing this. Until that moment we thought we were going to get a private boat trip to the dolphins, but now we understand that we have some company. Little did we know that this company will change our lives so much for the better. Shreya and I played a game at guessing the nationality of the couple who would be joining us on the boat. In December, Maldives was frequented by a lot of people from all over Europe and other cold territories of the world. So, Shreya guessed that the couple would be French. I went by statistical data and guessed they would be Russian. I knew from statistics that about one-third of the tourists visiting the Maldives in December are from Russia. As the couple approached the boat, we realised that we were both distantly off on our guesses. Sulekha and Promod, the names we knew a bit later and shall remember for life, were very much Indian and not European or Russian. Not only Indian, but they were also hardcore Marathi and hailed from Pen, a small town in interior Maharashtra.

'Hello, are you from India,' I asked Promod, trying to strike a conversation as the boat took off into the sea.

Promod smiled and nodded. He seemed a bit uncomfortable with us around.

'Are you on your honeymoon?' I asked Sulekha this time.

She giggled but nodded her head from right to left, indicating a strong no as an answer. They looked like they did not like much of a conversation. Shreya poked me, indicating me to stop poking them. But with my talkative and inquisitive nature, I found it difficult to travel with strangers on the same boat and not speak at all. I also observed another very strange element in the couple. Their body language, appearance, and attire did not make them look quite like tourists in the Maldives. Who dresses in an Indian saree on a boat ride on the Indian Ocean? They would probably be more fitting as tourists in Alibaugh or Agra.

'Which place in India are you from?' I asked, poking the man again, this time in Hindi.

'We are from Maharashtra?' the reply came from Promod in Hindi too.

I presumed that the couple was not very comfortable conversing in English. To give them even more comfort I threw my next question in native Marathi. Luckily with my years of working in plants in Maharashtra, I had mastered spoken skills in Marathi.

'Marathi ahe tumi (are you a Marathi)?' I asked.

The couple's eyes gleamed on hearing their mother tongue in the Maldives.

'Tumi pun Marathi ahe?' Sulekha exclaimed.

'No, we are not Marathi, but we live in Mumbai and speak the Language well?' I replied in Marathi again. With this lingual comfort, our conversation broke loose, mostly in Marathi and Hindi. In the next half hour, we came to know a lot of things about each other. And this conversation made all the difference to our future.

Promod and Sulekha were married for five years. They hailed from Pen Maharashtra where Promod ran a small grocery shop while Surekha worked as a surrogate mother to childless couples. This was the first time Shreya and I came to know of the term 'surrogacy'. Sulekha bore children for others who cannot bear the child themselves. The egg of the mother is implanted into Sulekha's womb where the child is nurtured for nine months. The procedure is very similar to the IVF procedure that Shreya and I had gone through earlier. The sperm of the father is copulated with the ovule of the mother to form an egg under laboratory conditions. The only difference being that post its formation, the egg is implanted into the uterus of a surrogate mother instead of the original mother. Post the pregnancy, Sulekha delivered the child, and then the child is handed over to the original mother. Sulekha in the last five years had already borne two such surrogate children. One for a lady whose uterus was damaged and could not biologically bear a child. The second child was for a star actress who did not want to take the risk of pregnancy marks on her own body. It was this actress who had shown her gratitude to Sulekha by sponsoring her a trip to the Maldives. This was Sulekha's first overseas vacation which she had won as a token of gratitude from this actress. It made sense to me now why she did not look like an apt tourist for the Maldives. Of course, Sulekha also got paid a hefty sum for her service rendered as a surrogate mother. Also, she is well taken care of by the original parents for whom she was bearing the child. Renting her womb was Sulekha's profession and the couple's main source of earning.

Shreya and I listened to Sulekha in awe. We never imagined that such a profession existed. Was this our ray of hope? Was this meeting with Sulekha planned by destiny? We just could not concentrate on watching dolphins or snorkelling the rest of the morning. We did not take a single snap the whole trip. My DSLR camera remained untouched throughout the trip. We could not take our minds off the 'surrogate mother' next to us. Shreya and I found a new silver lining towards becoming parents. On our boat ride back to the hotel, I took note of the contact details and addresses of Promod and Sulekha. First time during a vacation both Shreya and I wished that it was over soon, and we return to India so that we can pursue our dream once again. The rest of the three days of vacation we spent in the hotel business centre rather than the beach. We wanted internet access more dearly than a dive into the ocean. We did not have smartphones with ready internet access during that time and the hotel computer was our only way to research as much as we could on surrogate motherhood.

As soon as we were back in Mumbai, we got in touch with Doctor Kishori Kadam once again. Even after two years, she recognised us instantly. We told her about our plans for surrogacy. She agreed to it immediately. She also explained to us the detailed process. First, it involved a lot of legalities. A proper contract needed to be signed between us and the proposed surrogate mother regarding commercial arrangements and the final custody of the child. Second, it involved a hefty sum of money as apart from the cost of IVF it also involved the fees charged by the surrogate mother. Third, since surrogacy was still not so prevalent in Indian society, respective close family and relatives needed to be aligned to the idea. And finally, after all this, there was no guarantee that the child would form and survive in the surrogate mother's womb. It was an act of nature after all. Dr Kadam wanted us to think again before we proceeded with this step. But we had already done our thinking back in the Maldives. Without any hesitation, we wanted to go for surrogacy as soon as possible. Shreya and I convinced our respective parents of our idea. I spoke to Aarushi too, both for medical advice and also for her advice as an elder sister. She was overjoyed. So, Sulekha was contacted. All hers and our blood tests were done and the legal formalities were completed. The commercials were also taken care of. Shreya and I once again went through the already practised procedure of IVF and finally, our egg was planted into the uterus of Sulekha Mahadik. A long wait of nine months followed with innumerable trips to Pen and to see how Surekha was doing. Surekha also made quite a few trips to Dr Kadam's clinic to get checked on the progress of our child. Even more, trips were made to the Shirdi Sai temple where Shreya and

I prayed deeply for our success this time. The rest was history.

On the afternoon of 1st December 2011, Shreya and I found us waiting anxiously in the maternity ward of Jaslok Hospital, Mumbai. Sulekha was admitted here for delivering our child. As we waited outside the operation theatre, I remembered the day in Fortis Kandivali about three years ago. The good part was that this time Shreya was with me outside. And this time too Shashi and Shalini bunked the office and were with us. We all waited for the greatest news on earth. Every minute seemed like an hour. I had bitten off every piece of nail on all my fingers. It was a Thursday. In Maharashtra, it was believed Thursdays were the days of worship for Sai Baba. Nothing can go wrong with his devotees on a Thursday. And it did not go wrong for us too. The miracle happened. Exactly at 7.15 PM, Dr Kishori Kadam walked out of the OT to tell us the sweetest three words that Shreya and I had heard until that point in time.

'It's a boy,' said Dr Kadam, as she took off her gloves and walked past us.

Shreya and I hugged each other tightly, tears rolled down our eyes. Three years and three failures later we could hear those three words that we so desperately longed for. In fact, we were one of the rare couples who could share this moment of joy together. In a natural pregnancy, when the father hears of this news, the mother lies unconscious on the OT bed.

Thanks to this unique medium of a surrogate mother, Shreya and I could weep together with joy. Shashi and Shalini were overjoyed too. They congratulated us wholeheartedly. They were the first persons to share the joy with us even before our parents knew about the good news.

After two hours, we could see the baby Abhijeet for the first time. Yes, Shreya and I were prepared with two names well in advance. Abhijeet if he was a son and Abhilasha if she was a daughter. Abhijeet it was. He lay beside Sulekha, all covered in white with just the bright face showing up. He was sleeping with his eyes closed. Sulekha was still unconscious, probably in a trance of anaesthesia. Shreya could not control herself on seeing little Abhi. She wept relentlessly with joy. For the first time, I saw the GM supply chain of Unilever weeping like a baby. I bent down on Abhi and kissed his forehead gently. The bundle of joy was all ours now. I felt like offering a champagne treat to the whole of Mumbai at that moment. In my mind, I profusely thanked Sai Baba for this wonderful miracle.

The next year of life was eternal bliss. Both Shreya's and my priorities changed. Career and work were no longer our priority. We did not want to meet friends or party or go to a cinema on the weekends. We even did not check on our parents' health as often as we used to as a DINK couple. Our priorities revolve around little Abhijeet. What to feed him, what he will wear, how is his health, and so on so forth. Regular visits to the paediatric doctor increased. Not that Abhi was unhealthy, we became a bit too paranoid. Abhi, on the contrary, seemed to be a very happy child. Even as a baby he seldom cried. He fed himself well on Pediasure and Cerelac as Shreya could not breastfeed him. He slept tight in the night without disturbing us. We had heard so many tales from friends about sleepless nights nurturing a baby. Touchwood, we did not experience any such nights with Abhi. Shreya had opted for a six months maternity leave, but she chose to join back only after four months. We had kept a full-time nanny named Gitu to take care of Abhi as Shreya joined her office. Gitu and Abhi seemed to gel well together, while Shreya and I both came back home sharp at 6 PM to spend the rest of the time with our little son. Nothing mattered to us more than him.

Time flew as Abhi turned one and a half as he created memories for us. I personally captured his moments of growing up in my DSLR and made three fat albums on him. He still could not speak complete sentences or even words, but he started communicating with us through broken words and signs. It was a treat to see him starting to toddle around the whole house as he graduated from his crawling. I will never forget the first word he uttered – 'dada' he said calling out to me. As per my acquired knowledge, children usually call out to their moms as their first word. My experience was totally the opposite, and I was just overjoyed. Time and again, as a father, I recalled my days with dad. He used to always tell me, that when I become a father myself, I shall understand what a father meant. 'A typical cliché,' I thought. Today I realised its inner meaning. I missed him now when he was no more. How I wish he could see his grandson. The journey of fatherhood had just begun. So many responsibilities I would have to fulfill as Abhijeet grows up. I will have to teach him to walk, run, swim, and cycle just as my dad had taught me. I will have to give him the best education. Moreover, I will have to make a gentleman out of this little boy.

I picked up Abhijeet as he toddled towards me as soon as I returned from New York.

'Dada, dada, dada,' he went calling out to me insistently. Probably he too missed me when I was away for a full two weeks.

I hugged him and showered him with kisses.

———

Chapter 9

GOING TO GURGAON

(June 2014)

'This bedroom is too small,' I complained as the property broker showed me around the flat in Exotica Towers, Golf Course Road Gurgaon.

'This is not a bedroom sir, this is the servant room,' said the broker, laughing out aloud.

'You mean, a separate room for the servant or maid to stay?' I asked perplexed.

'Yes sir, the servant room also has an attached toilet for use of the servant,' he said.

I was still perplexed. With my thirteen years of living in Mumbai, I never heard of a servant room. In Mumbai, real estate was too expensive to accommodate servants in a separate room, and that too with a separate attached bathroom. It seemed Gurgaon was way different in that aspect. And that too, as per the broker, the flat he was showing me was a 'supposedly' small flat in Gurgaon. He was insisting that with my rental budget I should be looking for a five-bedroom villa or a bungalow. Akash, the broker, was unpleasantly surprised when I insisted on seeing three-bedroom apartments. He was evidently unaware of the real estate sizes in Mumbai. In Mumbai, we owned a two bed-room flat of 1000 square feet, which was a matter of pride. By Mumbai standards owning this size of a property in Borivali was not a mean feat. When Akash said that this three-bed penthouse administering 4000 square feet was small according to my standards, I fell from the sky.

'You call a four thousand square feet penthouse 'small' as per my standards? Who do you think I am? I am Abhinav Bhattacharya and not Amitabh Bachchan,' I told Akash.

'Sir, you have a rent budget of a lac. I can show you four-bed villas and five-bed condos in that rent,' replied Akash.

'What? A five-bedroom apartment in one lac of rent?' My jaws fell apart in surprise.

'Sir, don't compare Mumbai rentals with Gurgaon, they are topographically different places,' smiled Akash.

I still did not believe my ears. Gurgaon rentals and the size of the house were a pleasant surprise to me. How can Akash call 4000 sq feet flat as small? I wondered. Imagine, what I mistook for a bedroom was a servant room! My god! Nonetheless, Shreya, Akash, and I continued the rest of our reiki in the three-bed 'small' penthouse.

The flat was simply fabulous. Apart from the servant room, the first level of the penthouse had the kitchen which was double the size of our Mumbai Kitchen, the living room, a separate dining room, a bedroom, and two balconies. In our Mumbai flat, we had one balcony too, which was a luxury to have by Mumbai standards. But that balcony was in no comparison to the ones in this penthouse. In Mumbai terminology, these would be called terraces and not balconies. A spiral staircase on one corner of the dining room led to the second level of the penthouse. The second level of the penthouse was even more sprawling, with two bedrooms, each with an attached bath and balconies, a storeroom, a puja- room, and a terrace. In Shreya's words, this terrace looked large enough to accommodate a helipad. To me, the most fascinating part of the house was its bathrooms. There were five of them. One with the servant room, one in the living room for guests, and all three bedrooms had one toilet each. In Mumbai, only our master bedroom had an attached bathroom, apart from this there was only one small common bathroom that served the other room and living room together. In this flat, the bathroom attached to the master bedroom was of a size that only the rich and famous of Mumbai could afford. The bathroom had a jacuzzi tub, a shower enclosure, a separate enclosed commode area, and a huge washbasin with a full-size mirror. In my life, I had never walked into a bathroom so luxurious, not even in hotels. Shreya and I unanimously agreed to take this penthouse on rent, without even seeing other choices that Akash had scheduled for us to see. A four thousand square feet penthouse at a rent of seventy thousand was an unbelievable deal for us.

Thus, began our journey from 1000 sq feet flat in Borivali, Mumbai to a 4000 sq feet sprawling penthouse in the posh Golf Course Road in Gurgaon. It was because of my career move that we had to move cities. From a Regional Logistics Manager with PepsiCo in the West, I was promoted to Senior Manager of National Logistics, taking care of Logistics operation pan India for PepsiCo. This position was based out of the PepsiCo headquarters in Gurgaon and hence entailed shifting cities from Mumbai to Gurgaon. This position was offered to me earlier also, but I vehemently refused to shift my base from Mumbai. Ever since I had shifted to Mumbai from Kolkata thirteen years ago, I had fallen in love with 'amchi Mumbai'. I did not even want to go back to Kolkata, let alone any other city in the country. The thought of leaving the amazing magical city pained me. Moreover, Shreya was doing well in her career with Unilever and I did not want to have a split family life. But this time around, Shreya was keener for my accepting the promotion than I was.

'How will I leave you and Abhijeet and stay in a shitty place like Gurgaon,' I told Shreya.

'We will work out a solution, you don't keep on refusing promotions. How will you grow in career dear?' said Shreya.

'I give a damn to my career. I am happy where I am. I can't leave Mumbai and you,' I tried to sound romantic.

I had been to Gurgaon quite a few times on business meetings in the PepsiCo headquarters. I did not like the look and feel of Gurgaon at all. The city looked so morose. It lacked the life of Mumbai. The evenings here were dimly lit, probably because of the absence of roadside shops as well as streetlights. Unlike in Mumbai, there was no hustle and bustle, and no speed. Public transport facilities were also minimal. In a nutshell, I did not like Gurgaon at all. Amchi Mumbai was the best. But Shreya was not convinced at all.

'A city cannot decide our career Abhi, we have both left our hometown to make a career. And Mumbai is not our own. So, let's go to Gurgaon,' said Shreya.

'What do you mean- let's go. How will you go to Gurgaon?' I tried to dampen her spirit.

'I will figure it out,' she said.

And so, she did.

Within two weeks, Shreya could convince Unilever Management that she can manage her job from

Gurgaon. Though she was based in Mumbai, she had a national responsibility. Though most of her stakeholders were based in the HO of Mumbai, her teams were anyways spread in all parts of India. So, she could well manage her supply chain deliverables from anywhere. She would travel to Mumbai as and when required to attend important stakeholder meetings. The idea was a bit out of the box during that time (the world was not so virtual due to COVID, back in 2014). But Unilever was a very diversity-friendly company and could not dishearten a lady General Manager, hence they relented to the concept of Shreya working from Gurgaon. Hence, we were all set to move to Gurgaon as a family. We did not know that we shall soon fall in love with the luxurious living of Gurgaon.

The penthouse we finalised was our first brush with 'luxurious living'. Almost 3000 sq feet was added to our living at no extra cost. The rent we would be earning from our 1000 sq ft own flat in Borivali would be equal to the rent we negotiated for this penthouse. From bathing in a 50 sq feet bathroom to lying in a jacuzzi tub is what I called upgraded living. Shashi, Shalini, Amit, and Yogesh had come to see off at the Mumbai airport. Finally, with a warm farewell from our friends in Mumbai, we landed in Gurgaon in July 2014.

We took some time in being acquainted with the new city. Gurgaon was way different culturally, climatically, and topographically from Mumbai. The very first morning in Gurgaon, while using the lift, I got a taste of what I call the 'Hello' culture. As I entered the lift, there was an elderly woman already in it. Usually, in the lifts of Mumbai, co-passengers keep a straight face and do not talk to each other, unless they happen to know one another. Also, like Mumbai locals, Mumbai lifts are very crowded, and having only two passengers in a lift was very surprising.

'Good morning. How are you doing?' the lady in the lift asked me with a smile.

I was confused for a few seconds. Do I know her? I thought. Possibly not as we had just shifted in a day before. Then why was she asking how I am? Later as I graduated on Gurgaon living, I realised that this was the 'hello' culture. When you see someone in the lift or lobby, you say hello, irrespective of the fact you know the other person or not. 'Very polite of them,' I thought.

'I am fine Madam. How about you?' I replied with a smile. That's about all the word exchange we had in the lift.

Gradually, I realized that this 'hello' culture was just a coating of sugar on the extremely insensitive and stubborn nature of the people in North India. I realised this for the first time when Shreya, Abhijeet, and I went to Lotus Valley School for Abhi's admission. Every parent around was well decked up. Coats, blazers, gowns, and expensive Indian dresses were rampant. Unlike Mumbai, the people here seemed to have some taste of attire. In Mumbai, dressing up was a simple affair. No one around just had the time to look at one another, let alone bothering about what one was wearing. If one had the basics covered, any dress was fine to go out with. This school admission attires of the parents in Gurgaon could beat any wedding ceremony dressing in Mumbai. I felt a little shaky to be underdressed in just old jeans and a tee. As soon as the principal entered the room, I found out the next part of the Gurgaon culture. Every parent in the room, especially the mothers wanted first preference of admissions. Everyone tried to prove how important they were as compared to the others. Everyone seemed to be hard-pressed for time. We waited patiently for our turn to present our case to the principal and ultimately secured admissions for Abhijeet in Lotus Valley School. The ultimate taste of the culture I perceived was at the parking when I saw two fathers having a verbal duet in the parking lot over who gets to park at that spot. I saw absolutely no reason to fight, there was enough space in the parking lot for a hundred cars, but still, they chose to hit upon each other's ego on that solitary parking spot. I was concerned to think what children would learn from such arrogant parents.

As time passed, I saw and detested more with the 'people' culture of Gurgaon. I came across aunties who park their cars blocking the road while they shop vegetables from roadside stalls. I had once come out of my car to request one auntie to park her car a bit further away so that other cars can pass through. The aunty did not even look at me, she behaved as if I did not even exist. I felt like slapping her at that moment, but I controlled my anger and patiently waited for her to finish her carrot and brinjal shopping. I came across uncles who park their cars in such a way in the parking lot and go away that I could not take out my car till they came around and removed their cars. How can people be so insensitive to block other cars in the parking lot? I came across so many cars and bikes being driven on the wrong side that sometimes I wondered whether I was driving the right way. Road sense seemed to be totally absent on the Gurgaon roads. Luckily the roads were broad enough to give margin to such driving and avoid accidents. Everyone around seemed to be rich and famous in Gurgaon, the corporates, the businessmen, the doctors, and even the farmers.

Apart from the cultural aspect, Gurgaon had a lot of positives. It had luxury, space, and convenience which were totally absent in Mumbai. Our penthouse was a great example of spacious luxury. Also, the roads were wide, buildings were not breathing on each other. Unlike Mumbai, there was enough open space. One thing that Gurgaon had which Mumbai will never probably have was silence. In Mumbai, even though we were sleeping in a 20th floor bedroom, our nights were filled with numerous noises. Noise from Masjids and Mandirs around, noise from continuous traffic, the noise of dogs barking, and from many other sources. Our slumber was accompanied by these noises. The first few nights in Gurgaon, I just could not sleep due to the creepy silence. There was no noise at all making its way into my bedroom. I was so accustomed to sleeping in the thoroughfare of Mumbai, that this silence made me stay awake for some nights. Gradually I started loving this silence. The second thing which I loved about Gurgaon was the time it took to commute from one place to another. In Mumbai, Shreya used to travel for 15 KM from Borivali to her Head Quarters in Andheri and it took almost an hour. I travelled 25 Km and it took almost 90 minutes. In Gurgaon, Shreya covered 5 KM in 4 minutes to her office and I covered 15 KM in 15 Minutes flat. I personally found two and a half hours extra in the day, saved out of driving time. I loved it. I even had to change my exercise timings. Because of the weary travel in Mumbai, I only got time for a jog from 10 PM to 11 PM. In Mumbai, it was common to find joggers at that hour. When I continued the same timing in Gurgaon, trying to jog within the society at 10 PM, I was subjected to suspicious glances from the security guards in our complex. I had no option but to change my jogging timings to the morning hours. The sheer convenience of Gurgaon was gradually making us forget Mumbai.

We experienced the most amazing difference between Mumbai and Gurgaon five months after we shifted to Gurgaon in July. Then December approached. We almost experienced a European October, which was unthinkable compared to the sweaty, humid, and hot

Mumbai. I just loved the winter of the North. In fact, in Gurgaon, we realised that there were seasons called autumn and winter, in Mumbai, there were only two seasons – rains and summer. The temperature in the North hovered between five to fifteen degrees during December and January, making it just perfect. In fact, winters in the North were what most Mumbaikar's dreaded. On the contrary, the three of us enjoyed the climate. Though we had very few friends in the new city, still we hosted bonfires on our private terrace for whatever few acquaintances we had in town. Just imagine having a bonfire on a private terrace in Mumbai! Even when no guests were coming over, Shreya and I sat by the fire on our terrace on chilly winter weekends, sipping on single malts. Luckily, we possessed woollen wear which we used in our European vacations, unlike most Mumbaikars who would generally not possess any warm clothes suitable for the Gurgaon winters. Apart from the winters, I personally found summers in the north better than the extreme humidity of Mumbai summers. Moreover, the rains here were much less damaging than the rainy season of amchi Mumbai. In a nutshell, Shreya and I gave more marks climatically to Gurgaon than to Mumbai.

As time passed, we started to like our stay in the commercial capital of Haryana and missed the Indian commercial capital lesser and lesser. Gurgaon contributed to our luck on commerce too. I had anyways walked into the city with a promotion. Astonishingly, even while working remotely from

Gurgaon, Shreya grabbed one more promotion from Unilever, making her the Director of Logistics for Unilever India. Keeping up with the 'show off' culture of Gurgaon, Shreya changed her car to an Audi A4. I still trudged along to the office with my old Toyota Corolla which still had a Maharashtra number plate, probably the only remains from our life in Mumbai. When we shifted to Gurgaon, little did Shreya and I expect that we shall be having a long stay in this town and our little master will be growing up the Gurgaon way.

———

Chapter 10

DECIPHERING DADDYHOOD

(April 2016)

I was elated to see Abhijeet taking his first freestyle stroke across the large pool in our housing complex. I was swimming right beside him, as I guessed that he may not be able to cross the large Olympic size pool. Halfway down, Abhijeet lost his breath and stopped. I held him as he started panting for breath. He still looked happy to have accomplished the halfway mark of the pool. I was not just happy. I was elated to see my achievement of training my son to swim. I gleamed in the glory of being a proud father.

We shifted to Gurgaon when Abhi was less than three. Even in Mumbai, we the father-son duo did take plunges into the swimming pool on lazy Sunday afternoons. Abhi used to wear inflated balloons on his arms and paddle through the water. The problem with the swimming pool in Mumbai was that it was overcrowded on Sunday afternoons, giving little individual space to swim. The pools in this Gurgaon housing complex were way different. There were three large pools in our society, the largest one being almost a full-size Olympic pool. There was enough space in this pool to swim and let swim. It was in this pool that over the last one month I was training my four-year-old son to swim. On the 26th day of training, Abhijeet could finally do a clean freestyle stroke halfway down the pool. We were both proud as we left the pool and went towards the dressing room. He just could not wait to tell Shreya about his achievement.

As years passed by, Abhijeet gradually grew up in Gurgaon. There were two things in life which one needs to learn only once in a lifetime, and this knowledge stays ever after. Swimming and cycling. Both these skills I had learned from my father. I still cherish those memories of how he forced me into the cold waters of the Ganges against my will. And how he ran beside my trembling cycle, giving me confidence that he shall hold me if I fall. I wanted to pass on the same memories to Abhi as he grew up. I had already taught him swimming when he was four. Next on his fifth birthday, I gifted him a bicycle. It was now my turn as a father to run behind my cycling son. I did not allow Abhi to use the support wheels on his cycle. I became his support instead, holding the bike from behind as he started cycling. I felt young and fit as I ran behind Abhi on his cycle. Finally, on the seventh day, we both felt proud once again as Abhi cycled across the lawn and I stood by watching him. I could successfully pass on the life lessons of swimming and cycling to my son, just as my dad passed them on to me.

During Abhi's growing-up years, I deciphered what it meant to be a dad. My priorities changed. Career was no longer seemed as important to me as earlier. I avoided as many business travels as possible. The taste of Saturday night movies changed from the latest block blusters to Marvel movies. The channels on the living room television changed from CNN to Cartoon Network. Probably, I kicked a football after twenty years. I never played basketball after my college years, and then one fine day I was back at the court with Abhijeet. I felt I was reliving childhood through my child once again. Time and again I thanked Sulekha for giving us this wonderful gift. Probably, for her, it was just a profession and she did it for money. But for Shreya and me, she was an incarnation of God who gave us our child. I felt strange that Sulekha never contacted us again, neither did we do the same. As per our legal contract, Sulekha could never claim the child that she had given birth to. I found it a bit strange. How can a lady not get emotionally attached to a child that she had given birth to? Was the profession of surrogacy so commercial after all?

Another person I always remembered was my dad. Whenever I did not listen to him or went against his will, he always told me that I will only know how he feels when I became a dad. He was no more, but I started realising what his words meant. I told Abhi the same words when he was five. We were on a vacation to Los Angeles and I was trying to reason with him not to buy a specific toy. But he was adamant and nagging with me to buy that toy for him.

'You are not listing to me Abhi, I am feeling very sad,' I told him.

'I don't care, how you feel, I want the Captain America Model,' he answered.

'You will understand how it feels to have a nagging son when you become a father,' I repeated my dad's dialogue to my son.

I am sure he did not follow what it meant, but he kept silent for some time. Shreya, Abhijeet, and I were in the Universal Studios, Los Angeles. As Abhi was growing up, Shreya and I had to keep his priorities in mind while choosing a vacation spot. Somewhere where we could fulfill our agenda of a relaxing vacay, while Abhi could be kept excited about something he likes. With a lot of research, we found out such spots which could fulfill both criteria. Last year we visited France. This country had things of both the parent's and child's interest. While Abhi was excited to see Disneyland near Paris, we enjoyed the serene trip to Nice, South France. While he was excited to see the snow in the French Alps, we were happy to see the Monalisa in Louvre Museum. This time we chose LA, which could satisfy both our vacation needs. We enjoyed seeing the Walk of fame, the Hollywood, and Beverly Hills while Abhi was enjoying the trip to the Universal Studios. Truly speaking, Universal Studios was so mesmerising that both adults and children could enjoy it equally. It was in the souvenir shop of the Universal Studios that Abhi fell in love with a three feet model of Captain America. He was desperate to own that toy while both Shreya and I were hell-bent not to spend our dough on that thing. Firstly, it was a whopping 130 USD in price, and secondly carrying a three feet toy, all the way from LA to Gurgaon was no mean feat. We would surely have to fish out more dollars on excess luggage. But Abhi was in no mood to listen to logic.

'I want the Captain America, dada,' he kept on howling.

'Please dear, I can't buy you that one, why don't you look for other smaller size figures? See there is a small size Captain there on the shelf. You want that one?' I tried to divert his attention.

'No, I want that tall one only. Why can't we buy that one?' he was adamant.

'That Captain America is too big to go to India no?' I said.

'I don't believe you,' said Abhi.

'Abhi, it is too large to come into your suitcase, right,' I said.

'I shall carry it with me dada. Please, I will not leave Universal Studios without Captain America.'

'But how will the full grown-up Captain go to India with us, we don't have his plane ticket,' I said.

'I will carry on my lap, then he won't need a seat. I want it. I want it. I want it,' Abhi howled.

'We are not going to spend 130 USD on that stupid scarecrow. Get this loud and clear in your head Abhi,' Shreya intervened our father and son discussion with a burst of anger.

'Are we poor folks, that we can't spend 130 dollars?' Abhi asked.

'Abhi, please calm down, lets buy three small figures instead, one Spiderman one Captain America, and one Hulk, OK?' I tried my best to lure him away from the absurd toy.

'No. No. No. I want only that. I will not come with you if you don't buy me that toy,' he went on nagging.

First time in my five years with Abhi, I felt I was gradually losing patience. I felt like slapping him tight and pulling him away. Probably I would have done so by now if we were in India. Hitting even one's own child in American territory could have severe repercussions and I knew it. I tried to calm myself down. I bent down on my knees and took Abhi by his arms.

'Please Abhi, I can't buy you that,' I said.

Suddenly Abhi reacted in a way that he never did before. He punched me in my face.

'I want it. I want it. I want it,' he kept on shouting.

I lost it. I grabbed him tight and pinched him on his stomach. I pinched him instead of slapping him to avoid the public eye. Abhi howled in pain and tears burst out of his eyes. I picked him on my lap and left the shop as fast as I could.

As my anger subsided, remorse struck me hard. First time ever I hurt my own son physically. I felt like chopping off the fingers that pinched him. I remembered rare occasions when my dad had hit me. I felt how he must have felt then. When a father hits a child, he experiences more pain than the child. I learned that lesson that day. We were back on the train on our way to the Hotel. Abhi had slept on my lap after weeping for some time. He had realised by then that his father had betrayed him, and he won't get the toy. He would have been shocked to see his father hit him. I rest my head on the window of the subway train and wept silently through the journey. I cursed myself for not spending hundred dollars and buying him the toy. I wished I go back right then to the souvenir shop and buy Captain America for Abhi. I had almost made up my mind to do so, but Shreya stopped me. She was more a practical parent than I was.

'Oh, come on, he is just a child and would forget the toy by dinner,' she said. And we headed back to the hotel.

Life moved on with more joys around Abhi. He was six when he won his first elocution contest in his school. For the first time in life, I experienced how great it feels to see one's own child win. I had spent the whole of the previous evening teaching Abhi the verse for his elocution. I was overjoyed to see the fruit of my labour materialise as the winning prize for Abhi. Abhi was growing up into an all-rounder child, as most parents dream their child to be. He was pretty good in academics, he excelled in singing and elocution and unlike me, always won a place in the school choir. He was also good at karate and tennis. Shreya and I gleamed as proud parents. He also shared a strong bond of love with us. Of course, when we asked who Abhi loved the most, without thinking he selected his mom as his first choice. I came second on his list. But I did not mind that, Abhi was well above Shreya in my list of affection.

Every day when we went to bed, I hugged and kissed Abhi profusely. I could not remember when the last time my dad had hugged and kissed me. I made sure that Abhi remembers that I kissed him every day even if he was already six years old. We enjoyed our bedtime hugs. Abhi used to cuddle between Shreya and me in bed even though he was six years old. Most children at his age craved a room for themselves. Abhi also had a room for himself, decked up in his choice. The bedroom right next to our master bedroom was carved out to Abhi's choice. I had taken a personal interest in designing it on his sixth birthday. It had a huge television with a play station connected to it. Abhi used to love gaming on the play station which I gifted him on his birthday. The room was painted in a universal studio theme and decorated with pictures of all types of Marvel heroes. One wall had a huge glass cupboard that housed Abhi's favourite toys. Even the bed was specially designed in the theme of racing cars. Abhi just loved the room and spend a lot of time there. But he refused to sleep in it alone at night. Shreya cajoled him a lot, even tried to bribe him with new toys if he agreed to sleep alone. But Abhi won't budge. Right from his infant days, he cuddled in the night between us and refused to change that habit. Shreya went on coaxing him and even sometimes forcing him to go and sleep in his room, but with no result. I never coaxed him into sleeping alone. Deep inside, I knew that it would be difficult for me to sleep without Abhi by me. He acts as a natural contraceptive between us, I used to jokingly tell Shreya. But within me, I loved to be a small and happy family when it came to sleeping together on our king bed.

Time passed by. When we came to Gurgaon, neither Shreya nor I had intended to have such a long stay in Gurgaon. But it was already four years and Abhi had grown up to be seven. I gave him his first cell phone on his seventh birthday. Although Shreya was dead against gifting a phone to Abhi at this age, I just could not resist giving Abhi what he wanted the most.

'I love you Dad, you are the best dad in the world,' Abhi jumped around with joy as he opened his birthday gift.

He just could not believe his eyes. Of course, he was pretty sure that his dad would never disappoint him when it came to birthday gifts, but he could not imagine that his first-ever phone would be the latest model of the iPhone. He just could not wait to text all his friends from his new phone. In all his text messages he categorically mentioned he was texting from his iPhone. He was growing up to be a big 'show off' like his mom, I thought as I smiled in my mind.

That night, after Abhi's birthday bash, Shreya and I had a big fight over my gifting my son a phone.

'Who gave you the idea of giving Abhi a phone at this age?' Shreya frowned.

'What do you mean, don't I have the freedom of gifting my son what I like to?' I snarled.

'We should have at least discussed. As his mother, I have the right to know what you are gifting my son.'

'Come one, he is my son too, why are you fussing over what I gifted him?'

'Do you realise that you have opened the world of the internet to a seven-year-old?' she said.

'So what? Most of his schoolmates already have a phone?'

'What his schoolmates do is not our concern. I don't want to expose my son to YouTube videos and unlimited porno at this age?'

'Why are you assuming he would see porno? And how long can you resist him from the web? Today's kids can only be guided, not commanded Shreya,' I tried to reason with her.

But when Shreya is upset, she is beyond all reasons. Her snarls slowly graduated to roars and after a few more dialogues exchanged, that night's fight led us to sleep in different rooms. I retired in our bedroom with Abhi while Shreya banged the door of the guest room. By now Abhi had realised that when he found his parents sleeping in different rooms, it meant trouble. Abhi was already asleep by the time I came to bed alone that night. I kissed him as he turned around in his sleep. I kept awake for some more time, pondering over our fight.

Of late, I realised that we had been fighting way too often. Somehow after Abhi had arrived in our lives, he had become the priority for both of us. In the event, probably Shreya and I were no longer each other's point of interest. Was being parents taking us away from being a couple? We hardly thought about each other. We hardly talked about anything else but Abhi. We hardly took any couple time out anymore. We hardly even talked to each other. Our sex lives had pretty much reduced to once or twice a month, unlike our heydays a decade ago. 'Was this a natural fallback of becoming parents?' I wondered. Did we still love each other as husband and wife? Of course, we did. Still, Shreya and I were husband and wife. The only thing that changed was time. With time our love had almost become a habit and the romance had whizzed past us. Seeing each other every day, dining together, holidaying together, our morning walks together – everything had just become a mere habit. Probably Abhijeet was the only common interest left between the once intensely romantic Shreya and Abhinav. As I dozed off into my slumber, I hugged our little son and prayed that he always remained successful in holding his parents together on the same bed.

———

Chapter 11

THE 'R' IN ROMANCE RUNNING OUT

(September 2018)

'You can be a Director of Unilever, but I pay the EMI and run the house. To hell with your career,' I shouted at Shreya.

'I made the biggest mistake of my life by marrying a scoundrel like you,' she yelled back.

Smash! I picked up my dining plate and smashed it on the ground. It broke into pieces while scattering food all over the floor.

Shreya looked sternly at me. I looked back straight at her. Our maid, Aarti immediately stepped forward to clean the mess on the floor. I stood up from the dining table and headed to the bedroom and locked it from inside. Let the Director of Unilever find a bed for herself, I thought as I started changing into my nightwear.

'If you think you can do whatever you like, then please get out and find a different address,' shouted

Shreya from outside while banging on the bedroom door.

'I told you, the EMI for the house is still paid from my salary, so you please find a bedroom for yourself,' I yelled back as I crept into the bed, switching off the lights of the room.

I was still withering in anger. Over the last few months now, such brawls between Shreya and me had not been very infrequent. Was it her fault or mine? Probably both were at fault, but both refused to assess the situation from the other side of the table. Both of us had our list of complaints against each other. We argued over everything in everyday situations. Be it in a morning walk, dining out, or even during our vacations. In Shreya's words, both ends were not matching with each other. The relationship seemed to be slipping away every day and every moment.

Each morning, as a routine over the last four years, Shreya and I took an hour-long walk on our society lawn. We lived in an ultra-posh urban society in Gurgaon which offered a sprawling two-acre lawn to its residents. This one hour of the walk was the only time in the day that we two busy corporate professionals could speak to each other. Our next meeting of the day happened directly at the dinner table after returning from work. And that too, if none of us were traveling, which hardly was the case. Many times, during our official travel, we did not speak for three to four days at a stretch. So, whenever we both were in town, we used this one-hour morning walk to tell each other why our marriage was not working. What exactly was wrong with the other person.

Well, let's first talk about Shreya's version of the story, before we come to my side of the coin.

Shreya was ambitious and wanted her partner to be over-ambitious. She always dreamt of her husband being a super successful corporate CEO, and I was just a petty Senior Manager with PepsiCo. She wanted her husband to be superiorly well-groomed. She always wanted to see her hubby going to the office in a proper blue suit, white shirt, and even with cuff links on the shirt. On the contrary, I went to the office in a jeans and tee, which in most cases were not washed for a week. How else could I have taken advantage of the casual American culture at Pepsi? She detested my sense of style. She was factually right. I did not have a sense of style at all. I did not mind what I was wearing. And I was like that right since birth. If she did not notice it at the time when she agreed to marry me, I could not help her now. This was one part of her complaint, regarding my career ambition and dressing sense.

The second part of her dislike towards me was due to my utter middle-class mentality and lack of aristocracy. How could I be equally excited about a holiday in Shimla and a one in Seattle? How could I still have my hair cut in cheap wayside salons while she went to the most upmarket luxury salons of the city? In other words, how could I pay only eighty bucks for a hairdo, when she paid eight thousand. How could I look for cheap bargains while shopping? Why did I search the Amazon website for package deals and discounts, while she shopped from the most expensive stores in the most up-market DLF malls in Gurgaon? Why was I still satisfied driving a seven-year-old Toyota Corolla to the office, while she just upgraded her car to a new Merc E class last month? So, basically, what I called simplicity, she defined as being just middle class. What I defined as being true to our roots, she defined as the absence of style. Putting it more in a financial way, while I loved to invest money to grow it, Shreya loved to spend it on lifestyle and deplete it.

The third aspect of her complaint was my absence of romance. The same lady who found me extremely romantic when we married and moved to Mumbai complained that I have lost the R of romance fifteen years down the line. Yes, I did not offer her 40 roses on her fortieth birthday for sure. Neither did I buy her a diamond on our 15th anniversary, but that's not the way I define romance. To be fair to her, she also did not define romance as getting expensive gifts. She had some other definitions, such as a drive in the rain, holding hands in the movie theatre, taking abrupt selfies together, and many other idiotic ways of showing that we love each other. Now, factually I was already middle-aged, and taking a drive in the rain looked to be more painful and risky to me than being romantic. Holding hands in a public place felt more embarrassing than lovely. And trust me, forty roses cost a fucking bomb. So, my definition of showing romance to my better half was about keeping the house in order, paying the utility bills and tuition fees on time, spending the Saturday nights together. And last, but not least, we still slept on the same bed, though snoring on the bed had become more common than sex.

As per Shreya's definition, I was a total of a middle-class, ambitionless, monotonous, and unromantic partner.

Now let us turn the rolls and see the relationship from my shoes. I truly did not have any complaints about Shreya. The only aspect I hated was her constant endeavour to change my personality. Yes, I was a simple man. I did not want to flaunt off a style with branded suits and ties. I was not ambitious at all in my career and was blissfully happy with a cosy job in a major multinational. I was happy to be just a manager and possessed neither the ambition nor the ability to become the CEO of PepsiCo. I still earned decent enough to offer an above-average lifestyle to my family. One may call me a miser, but I detested paying thousands for a haircut when it could decently happen in a hundred. I personally believed that only a person of unsound mind can take his or her own photograph and so I always ran away from the event of taking selfies. I deeply felt that when the food was served on the table the fork should attack it first and not the mobile cameras. I kept away from social media glares as I respect my own and my family's privacy. What mattered to me most in vacation was that we spent time together as a family. I did not care whether the vacation was in Manali or Miami. It was important whether we as a couple like the vacay than how many likes registered on Instagram. That's the way I was and will always be. Shreya needed to understand that and accept me that way. Either she had changed her expectations about me with time or I had misunderstood her expectations fifteen years ago. As Shreya grew up from a simple executive in a logistics firm to a Director in Unilever, what grew along is her arrogance. And she probably never realised it. The moment she started mixing our individual identities with professional designations, our relationship gradually started drifting apart. The respect that a husband could claim from a wife fifteen years ago could not be claimed by a Sr Manager of PepsiCo from the Director of Unilever.

The silver lining in all our arguments during the morning walks was that we kept walking on together. Yes, plates did smash in the dining room and bedroom doors were locked with only one person inside, but the family room kept the lights burning. I never wanted to leave my family, probably neither did Shreya. Probably it was the common bonding for Abhijeet that had kept our parental relationship still going. Whether we liked being husband and wife or not, we always kept on being the mother and father to Abhijeet. So, our anniversaries also kept coming along with Abhijeet's birthdays. Our married life kept on trudging along. I kept on tolerating Shreya's arrogance and she reciprocated by tolerating my simplicity.

Nonetheless, our brawls never lasted long. Both of us were busy in our own careers and quickly forgot the family issues as we started dealing with corporate issues the very next day. This time too, as usual, we moved on with our daily life the very next day. I got up a bit late the next morning, it was already 8.30 by the clock. For a few seconds, I wondered why Aarti had not served me tea at seven. Then I remembered that I had locked the bedroom door last night after the brawl. I slowly got out of bed, unlocked the master bedroom door, and came out to the dining hall. Shreya was already at the table having her breakfast. She was set to leave for office. She must have slept in the guest room yesterday. Going by the clock, Abhijeet would have already left for school. I repented not dropping him off at the bus stop, which I always did when I was in town. That reminded me that I was not in town for the next three days.

'Aarti,' I called out to the maid.

'Yes Sir,' she promptly walked out of the kitchen.

'I shall be leaving for Chennai today evening and shall be back only on Friday evening,' I told Aarti in a voice loud enough so that Shreya could also hear.

I promptly glanced at Shreya just to make sure she heard, but she did not show any response to my words to Aarti. She calmly finished her fired egg and got up from the table.

I went back to the bedroom. I was too late to hit the gym now, moreover, I had to get ready and pack my bags for my Chennai trip that evening. I opened the closet to pack my bags for Chennai. I pulled out a small one-nightery trolley, though the trip was for three nights. I smiled at the thought that Shreya would have started yelling if she saw me travel with just three T-shirts, one pair of jeans, two undies, and two pairs of socks on an official trip. What else should I have carried on a factory visit? I don't attend board room meetings like Unilever Directors, I would have snapped at her. In fact, packing was one of the reasons where we started to fight before every family vacation. While I was a typical hippy packer, carrying a backpack across the globe, she would carry two designer wears per day multiplied by the number of days in the vacay. Which mathematically summed up to 2 thirty kilo bags for her, one fifteen kilo bag for Abhijeet, while I was good enough with a seven-kilo backpack which went as hand luggage.

'Shreya, why do you need a sixty-kilo suitcase for a two-week vacation? Thirty dresses, five pairs of shoes, three overcoats and so many cosmetics?' I would snap at her. And this was enough to arouse the fire in her.

'I don't travel like a beggar as you do' she would snap back at me.

'And who do you think will carry these suitcases halfway across the globe? I am not Hulk,' I would say.

'You don't have to carry my suitcases, I shall manage them,' she would say. But I was ultimately the one who had to do the herculean task of towing her luggage on most vacations.

But the brawl of over baggage was only the tip of the iceberg. The differences and frowns would continue right through the vacation over petty things. Food was one such thing – our choice of food varied, I liked European steaks while she would look for an Indian restaurant in Rome. The mode of travel was another such point of difference. When in Rome I behaved like the Romans and wanted to use public transport. She, on the other hand, detested it and hailed city cabs, which of course was brutally expensive, throwing my travel budget out of gear. But even after all this, luckily, we still did our vacations together. Though Shreya had proposed many times that we should try doing separate vacations with separate partners on separate continents, I never relented to the idea. It was our vacation to Italy last year October, that we almost decided not to be traveling again together. The whole of the vacation we just spent quarrelling and cursing our fifteen years of history, so much so that even little Abhijeet was fed up.

'I will never come on a trip with you guys again. I would be happy staying with Aarti didi at home and playing on the play station with my friends,' he said.

Even the little child's agony did not prompt us to stop our brawls. Ultimately on the last evening of our vacation, we had a major fight. That too, over a petty thing – why did I order my fourth peg of single malt. We were in a picturesque town on the Amalfi coast, sitting in a lovely open-air restaurant by the sea. Dusk had just fallen on an October evening. The serene waters of the sea and the chill in the air made a perfect romantic setting.

'Why did you order one more peg Abhi?' shouted Shreya loud enough to make the whole restaurant turn their attention to our table.

'It's such a lovely place Shreya. Just enjoy the serenity and don't fuss over my drink.'

'Can I enjoy the serenity with a drunkard?' came her reply.

'Just four pegs make me a drunkard, Shreya?' I snapped back at her.

A few more altercations followed. In the end, she banged the table and left for our hotel, taking Abhijeet along with her. The rest of the evening I kept on drinking alone in one of the most romantic places on earth. I don't remember how many shots I gulped down that evening. I wept alone as I drank. Was the R in our romance gradually falling apart? I thought. Have we reached a point to end the relationship? Will only being Abhijeet's parents give us fuel enough to drag our married life ahead? Will the little mind of Abhijeet be able to accept it if we got divorced? Should we pull the plug or try and trudge on? Many questions went across through me on that October evening on the Amalfi coast. Finally, I came to one conclusion that at least we will not go on a vacation together again. Our normal corporate routine keeps our minds and body diverted on most weekdays. Probably being busy was a boon to Shreya's and Abhinav's marital life and we should not be taking time off together again. But will this trick be long-lasting? How long can we carry on? I pondered as I started walking back to our hotel that evening.

'Should I prepare your breakfast Sir?' asked Aarti knocking on the bedroom door. My chain of thoughts came back to the present. I closed my packed suitcase, all set to spend the next three days away from Shreya.

'I am going for a shower, keep breakfast on the table in twenty minutes,' I replied to Aarti.

The only person I missed during my official trips away from Gurgaon was Abhijeet, I thought as I walked into the shower. Thanks to him that Shreya and I were still together.

———

Chapter 12

Breaking the Bank Account

(January 2019)

'Have you gone nuts Shreya? You just blew off ten fucking lakhs?' I yelled at the top of my voice.

My voice was so high-pitched that even our two maids ran out of the kitchen to see what was wrong.

'That's my money Abhinav, who the fuck are you to ask me about it?' Shreya yelled back with equal magnitude.

'It has been years since we agreed that there is nothing called 'my money' between us, right?' I said.

'But I earned it,' said Shreya after a short pause.

'That does not mean you can waste ten lakh worth of rupees?' I shouted again.

'Stop shouting, okay? Ten lakhs are less than just my share pay out this year. First, earn as much a salary as me and then shout,' Shreya vent out.

'Earning a share of ten lakhs does not give you the right to donate the amount to your good-for-nothing boyfriend,' I snarled back as I flung a book across the room. The book was the first thing I could lay my hands on to vent out my anger.

'I don't need to ask you before I use my money Abhinav. I earn more than you.'

It is at this comment that I have no option but to retreat from any heated argument with Shreya. Every monetary discussion is put an end to with the same dialogue. Yes, I am a senior manager while she is a director. This fact is kept in front of me every time, almost every day. But I am no male chauvinist. I have always respected and encouraged the fact that my wife is more successful than me. The point is I did not get any respect in return. Moreover, the fact of her making more money than me did not justify her donating ten lakhs to Dipankar, her ex-boyfriend. Apparently, Dipankar was starting a business and was running short of capital and he approached Shreya for help. Shreya gleefully gave the bugger the money. Of course, she had been convinced that the money would come back once the business started generating revenue. I was relatively certain that the opportunity of the money coming back won't come very soon. Of course,

Shreya did have the right to do anything she likes with her money, I do not doubt that. I only felt bad about two aspects, first, she did not consult me at all, and second, the money was paid to Dipankar. Probably it was because she was helping Dipankar, she did not consult me.

Dipankar was Shreya's boyfriend during her college days. I was not very certain as to why their relationship had not worked out. Neither did I show much of an interest to know about the same. Even after marriage, she had kept intermittent contact with Dipankar. I can't honestly say that I did not mind it, but I did not come in the way too much. In fact, I also met Dipankar a couple of times after our marriage. Once when Dipankar had come to our house for coffee, and another time when I met him at a common friend's get-together. He was also happily married and lived in Bangalore with his wife and son. Shreya occasionally spoke to him, chatted up, and perhaps also met sometimes. But I was not exactly a spying husband. I too had two affairs before marriage, the first one was with Shreelekha, during my school days, and the second with Twinkle during my college years. I had come clean with Shreya about both these cases. I had physical relations with both these women in my heydays, unlike Shreya who claimed that she never got physical with Dipankar. I did not deep dive much. Jokingly I used to tell her that probably Dipankar was gay, else he would not have missed such an opportunity.

After marriage, I had social contact with Shreelekha only through our Facebook and Instagram accounts. A cordial message exchange happened during each other's birthdays and festivals such as Holi, Diwali, and New year. That was about it with Shree, we did not have any personal contact. We had a chance to meet at Delhi airport once, though only by chance. She was traveling back with her family from a holiday while I was coming back from an official trip from Delhi to Mumbai. It was just an unplanned bump-off at the Delhi airport lounge. I probably saw Shree after twenty years that day. We talked a bit about our present and our past over a coffee at the lounge. But somehow, I did not feel the same excitement about seeing her as I used to twenty years ago. Probably in my mind, I was still holding the image of Shree in her teens, a bubbly, energetic, pretty damsel. When I met her after years, she had mellowed down to almost a middle-aged lady in her early forties, and not the Shreelekha who was inscribed on my memory. Nonetheless, we exchanged phone numbers and graciously parted as we boarded our respective flights. We never used the phone numbers ever after the chance meeting.

With Twinkle, I had no contact at all. Right from the time we left college, Twinkle had totally vanished. In those days we did not have cell phones so there was no way to contact her. I also moved on in life with my post-graduation and my job thereafter and forgot all about the lovely sleepovers with Twinkle. I owed a lot to Twinkle in helping me out of depression after my breakup with Shree. Probably, I would have drowned myself with Vodka and Marijuana had it not been for Twinkle. My sex life was on roll in my twenties, all because of her. She was a roar when it came to sex. Much later, I did try to search her on social media, but could not find any trace of her. Probably Twinkle Fernandez was not a Fernandez anymore. But I had never hidden anything from Shreya.

I told her about my meeting with Shree on the very evening I had met her in the Delhi airport lounge. But somehow Shreya kept me under the scanner of her doubts. I knew that she sometimes checked my phone too. In fact, even my phone unlock password was not a secret I kept from her. I did not reciprocate in the same manner though. I never checked on her, though I know she had maintained contact with Dipankar. I did mind it somewhere deep inside me but did not want to curb her freedom. I trusted Shreya to the fullest. But today, I just could not digest the fact that she gave away ten lakhs to Dipankar. Truly speaking, had she asked me, I would have prevented her from deploying such a sum of money to any start-up venture. It was hard-earned money and should not have been wasted like this. I felt hurt at the fact that she did not even ask me before doing this transaction. Since we had a joint bank account with ICIC Bank where we both transferred our salaries, I got to see the transaction of ten lakhs. That's how I challenged her. But yes, the logical side of me told me that she did have the right to spend her money the way she wanted. Had the time come to separate our bank accounts? I wondered. At least I can be spared of repeated taunts from Shreya for earning less than her.

It was not only about the money or our respective corporate positions, many other factors off late were creating a rift in our sixteen years of relationship. Shreya was very vocal about her dislikes. She disliked me being an ordinary individual. For her, anyone below the rank of General manager in the corporate sector was an ordinary individual. So, as Senior Manager, I was almost non-existent. To add to that, my sense of style and my taste were also ordinary. I drove an ordinary car, I wore ordinary clothes, I drank ordinary wine, and so forth. Even our choice of vacation spots was gradually becoming contradictory. She wanted to go to elite and glamorous holiday destinations such as Miami, South France, Scotland, et al, while I wanted to explore the world by going to places like Alaska, Argentina, Antarctica, etc. Even when we firmed up a destination, the choice of hotels caused a rift between us. She wanted to stay at expensive branded hotels while I was happy with a simple bed and breakfast. I wanted to live within a budget while she was a spendthrift wife. Even her clothes had labels of Gucci, H&M, and Louis Vuitton while I was satisfied with clothes brought from Walmart stores. Gradually we understood that our relationship, like our choices, was standing poles apart.

Shreya was not like this when we married. Success and time were changing her, while I remained the ordinary Kolkata boy. In her words, her change was towards the better and there was nothing wrong with it. The more tried to convince her, the more arguments occurred. At times I lost my cool and had major duels with Shreya. As a father I realised that this was not having a good effect on Abhijeet, hence I fell silent. I stopped protesting and tried to stay as far apart from arguments as possible. As a result, our conversations had also stopped. Except for very necessary stuff, we hardly spoke. We were more becoming like spouses now, and not friends like our earlier times. Our physical intimacy also started going down and almost became a cordial monthly affair as time passed by. Was this normal after close to two decades of staying together? I had no one to whom I could ask this question and I kept on pondering within myself. Love was more becoming a habit to us now than a romantic bond. Our staying together was becoming a routine more than anything else. Probably a brief period of staying apart might help. I guessed.

'We need to separate our bank accounts,' said Shreya the next morning.

As usual, after our last night's duel over the ten lakhs, we had slept in separate rooms. Shreya came into my room and threw the statement at me. I had just about got up from sleep and for a few seconds could not place the sudden comment. Then I remembered last evening's altercation and sat straight on the bed. Shreya was thinking the same as I thought of last night.

'Yes, certainly. Our banks must break,' I replied.

'How do we do it, I mean how do we know how much money belongs to me,' said Shreya.

I was rather amused at the question than angry. After all this, she is coming with a calculator to calculate her share of the bank account.

'Well, there is a legal way and an amicable way,' I said with a smile showing my unbrushed teeth.

'What do you mean Abhinav, I am serious.'

'So am I. The legal way is that we hire a Chatter Accountant to audit our bank transactions for the last sixteen years, figure out who transferred how much, and who withdrew how much. Then draw up a balance sheet to ascertain how much of the liquid asset is yours and how much is mine,' I said in one breath.

'Sounds pretty complicated,' said Shreya as she sat down on the bed.

'Well, there is a simple amicable way, if that cheers you up,' I said.

'And what is that?'

'We transfer the money from our joint bank account in 50:50 ratio into our single bank accounts. Thereafter your money stays your money. None of us will transfer our salaries into the joint account anymore,' I explained.

'Then what happens to the joint bank account?'

'It becomes empty, and eventually, we can visit the nearest ICICI bank and close the account. Then each of us can enjoy separate financial freedom,' I said as I got out of bed, heading for the washroom.

'Why 50:50, I have always earned more than you Abhinav?' Shreya's question made me stop midway between the bed and the bathroom.

'You have a point madam, but you are forgetting that you have also spent more than me from the same joint account.'

'What is that comment supposed to mean?' Shreya seemed annoyed.

'Very simple, dear. Your car loan goes out of this account, your hefty credit card bill is paid from this account, your driver's salary is paid from this account,' I replied.

'Are the car and driver only mine?' said Shreya standing up now, preparing for another heated argument.

'Of course, they are, my car is fully depreciated, and I don't use a driver.'

'But it's a family asset, Abhijeet also uses it', snarled Shreya.

'He can also use my old car. You are spoiling him with luxury. Also, your credit card shopping bills are the heaviest amount that goes out of the account every month, I don't use credit cards at all, you see.' I said, with a fairly raised voice now.

'Can we split the account in a sixty and forty ratio, please?' said Shreya.

'Are you trying to negotiate with me?'

'What's wrong if I do, negotiations are part and parcel of both of our jobs,' Shreya gave a sarcastic smile.

'Well then, I am not game for it, it's either 50:50 or we can get the account audited.'

'You always claim you are a simple man, what are you going to do with the money, let's split it sixty-forty no,' continued Shreya, holding my palm.

'Don't try to get romantic, I am not going to leave the lion's share for your boyfriend. In fact, we should be deducting the ten lacs from your share,' I said.

'Ok then, let's go for 50:50. When do we do the transaction?' Shreya relented.

'I am running late for the office now, we can do it this evening after dinner,' I proposed and went inside the bathroom without waiting for Shreya's answer.

As I opened the tap of the washbasin, I could hear Shreya's bumping footsteps leave the room in haste. That day, I found it difficult to concentrate on work in the office. Memories flashed in my mind. I remembered the day when Shreya and I visited the ICICI bank Borivali branch to open our joint account. We both had our own salary accounts with CITI bank. I was the one who proposed that we should have a joint account where we transfer both our salaries every month. In that way, the money shall lose its identity of who earned it and shall become a common fund for our family. All our needs would be met by this account and money shall never come in the way of our relationship. Shreya was more than happy to relent to my idea. She felt it was a perfectly romantic idea to blend our earnings into one. All through the last sixteen years, we have satisfied all our family needs from this joint corpus. We event sent money home to our respective families. We paid all our grocery expenses, our vacations, Abhijeet's school and tuition fees, our home and car EMIs, our credit card bill, salaries, all from this one account. Although both of us could access this account without the help of the other, we never questioned any transaction made by each other. Our money had truly lost its identity as Shreya's earnings or mine. With our hard work and God's grace, our joint account had handsomely grown with time. It had close to sixty lacs of liquid cash now, apart from other investments in shares and funds. This account never came under the scanner until this morning when we proposed to break it. Times, they were certainly changing.

'How much do we have in the account, Abhi?' Shreya asked.

We were sitting in our study after dinner. As proposed in the morning, we were to settle the joint account today after dinner. Right through the day, I was just hoping that Shreya would forget the incident. I was mentally prepared to forget the fact that Shreya gave away ten lacs in loan to Dipankar. I just did not want to break down a sign of true love. I was afraid if I tell Shreya about my thought not to break the account, she might get me wrong. She might feel that I was not breaking it to have control and visibility of her money. So, I quietly hoped that Shreya would forget about the morning's incident. Unfortunately, that did not happen. Right after dinner, Shreya insisted that we sit in the study and settle accounts. While Abhijeet retired to bed, I opened my laptop and logged into our ICICI bank joint account.

'We have fifty-eight and a half lacs in cash and another ninety lakhs in shares and funds,' I replied to her question coldly.

'So, a total of one crore and forty-eight lac rupees. This means we get seventy-four lacs each.' Shreya seemed excited.

'Financially, I would recommend that we keep the shares and funds untouched and pull out the liquid fifty-eight lacs only. We can leave the fifty grants in the account to keep the account live. Unless you need all the cash to help Dipankar, don't pull out the long-term investments,' I said.

My comment had made Shreya visibly angry.

'Since you are taking custody of your money, who are you to give financial advice to me?' she shouted.

'I was not the one who proposed to break the account Shreya, it was you who wanted to do this. Nonetheless, I would still advise keeping the funds intact for Abhi's future education purposes,' I said.

I knew Shreya had a soft corner for Abhi's education and she will soften down if I bring this point in.

'Ok,' said Shreya, 'We can transfer twenty-four lakhs each,' she relented.

'Ok, we can affect the transfers tomorrow in the banking hours,' I said.

'Please do so and confirm to me,' said Shreya as he got up from the chair.

'Not so fast madam, now with the joint account gone, we have to chalk out who bears which expenses,' I said.

'What do you mean?'

'I mean, all these years you never understood how to run a family financially. EMI, electricity bill, school fees, tuition fees, driver salary, maid salary all had to be paid. All these were paid by me from our joint fund. Now we have to decide among ourselves who pays what so that we pay the family expenses equally.'

'Do you have a plan,' Shreya asked.

'Not exactly, I guess you pay your car EMI, I can pay the house EMI.'

Last year we purchased the same house in Gurgaon that we initially rented. So, our rent pay-outs got converted to house EMI.

'You can pay for Abhi's school and tuition and I can pay the maid and driver salaries. We can chalk out something similar,' I explained.

'We can do that tomorrow honey, I am extremely sleepy now,' said Shreya as she left the study.

'Don't forget to transfer the twenty-four lakhs into my CITI bank account tomorrow morning,' her voice drifted into the study as she shut the door of the bedroom.

I sat alone in the study, staring at the account statement on my laptop. Was this breaking up of the bank account the early signs of our breakup? Or was I just being a bit over-emotional?

———

Chapter 13

THE MAGIC OF MANJARI

(June 2019)

My fingers rolled over Manjari's back, desperately trying to unhook her bra. In the last sixteen years of marriage, I have never unstrapped any bra other than Shreya's. And over the last few months, ever since I moved back to Mumbai, I had run out of practice even with Shreya's undergarments. Our marital relation had almost lost the flavour of physical intimacy.

I kept on trying to unstrap Manjari's bra. At last, my fingers lost patience, and pulled the straps of Manjari's black bra down her shoulders. Her shapely pair of breasts bared themselves for my taking. I clutched them with both fists fondling them over and over. Soon my tongue joined the act to help my fingers. Manjari's taut nipples announced that they were enjoying their moments too.

I had moved to Mumbai in March this year following a west zonal assignment from PepsiCo. This is the point of life where I met Manjari. Moving to Mumbai was my choice. I could have easily resisted the promotion and the transfer that came along with it. Somehow, I embraced it instead. As my relationship was becoming tougher and tougher with Shreya, I felt staying apart for some time would help bring some peace for both of us. I felt this was a perfect chance of a near-permanent separation, camouflaged under the realms of career progression. This wilful separation can benefit us in either of the two ways. First, it would keep us away from our daily brawls and complaints and hence bring peace of mind to both of us. In that way, in the eyes of society we stay a happy and successful couple while internally, we keep our relation as parallel rails in two different cities, without much of an intersection. Probably we both can stay happily ever after. Second, the separation may also yield different results. We may start missing each other and think about rekindling our sour relationship. We might go back to times when we considered ourselves the most romantic couple around. Sometimes, too much togetherness causes couples to take each other for granted. Probably this separation could help us understand each other's importance through our absence.

Of course, going by my nature, I could not decide on moving to Mumbai without discussing it with Shreya. No matter how much she detested me, she was my wife. My leaving home could hamper a lot of things that she did not realise. Who would drop Abhijeet at school? Who would take care of Abhijeet when she was traveling? Who would do the grocery shopping?

But Shreya whipped off all my concerns in a jiffy. She was visibly elated with my career progression and did not want to come in the way of it. She agreed to my moving back to Mumbai at once. Did she detest me so much? Or was she so career-oriented that my promotion mattered more to her than my presence? I was sincerely confused. Not that I was not happy with my promotion, but I was more a family man than a corporate professional. The thought of leaving Shreya and Abhijeet alone was pinching me. But Shreya seemed to be well prepared for the feat.

'Would you be able to manage the house alone Shreya?' I asked.

'What do you mean by that Abhi?' she questioned back.

'I mean who would take care of Abhijeet when you go for official trips and I am in Mumbai? All these years we have maintained that we shall not travel out of town at the same time?' I explained.

'Aarti will take care. Abhijeet has grown up enough to manage', said Shreya.

'Who would drop him at the school bus stop?'

'I will,' came her brief reply.

'And when you are not in town?'

'What are we paying a driver for?' said Shreya.

'What about weekly grocery shopping?'

'Don't ask stupid questions in the era of online shopping. You think about your career, I shall manage. If you plan a long sting in the West, I can also join you next year in Mumbai and we move back as a family to Mumbai,' she said.

She was right, her company headquarters was situated in Mumbai, so if I plan to have a long stint in the West Zone then we can all move back to Mumbai.

So finally, I accepted the promotion offered by PepsiCo and went on to become the General Manager Sales for West zone, based out of Mumbai. We planned that initially, I go alone to Mumbai, and probably next year after Abhijeet's academic session we move as a family. That is if Shreya and I still decided to stay as a couple.

Within weeks, I started feeling that I had taken the right decision. I began to enjoy my newfound freedom in Mumbai. I circled back with old friends whom I had lost touch with ever since I left Mumbai and moved to Gurgaon. And in the era of social media, it was easy to get connected and announce my advent into Mumbai. On my first weekend in Mumbai, I posted my arrival back to 'amchi Mumbai' on my Instagram handle. Shortly Amit contacted me. I was elated. Soon enough, I found myself in a local bar along with Amit and Yogesh. We had not met since the days when we worked for Coca-Cola. I moved on to Pepsi while they still stuck on to Coca-Cola. I loved the evening out with them relishing old memories. How could we forget that July 2005 evening when we were stuck in the flood at Dahisar? We went on chatting and drinking through the evening like in our old times. We never realised when the clock struck midnight. With the time in the clock, I sensed that I was enjoying my freedom. Had this meeting with Amit and Yogesh been in Gurgaon, by now I would have had relentless calls from Shreya to get me home. Today, with my separate existence, I became the master of my own choice. I had no qualms drinking with friends till midnight, there was no one in my service apartment waiting for me. The question that crossed my mind was whether 'no one waiting for me' was a good thing or bad?

My tongue was done with Manjari's breasts and reached for her lips. While we locked our lips, I tried to remember when was the last time I had a French kiss? Shreya did not like it and did not do it too often. As Manjari's and my lips locked together, my hands reached for her jeans. By now my fingers had found their old form and swiftly unplugged Manjari's jeans buttons and zip. Slowly my right palm found its way deep inside her panties.

The weekend after my meeting with Amit and Yogesh was even more fascinating. I caught up with my old bachelor day roomies Chirag and Shashi. Chirag was down from Boston to Mumbai that week while Shashi was still working in Mumbai. This time the drinking session was even more nostalgic than the one with Amit and Yogesh. We talked through the evening about our old bachelor days. What not have we done as bachelor boys. We talked about our times in the two-room flat in Kalyan. How we enjoyed our daily train journey from Kalyan to our tile factory in Thane. How we detested our cold dinner dabbas which were placed in front of our flat every day. (The reference of these stories can be found in my book *Lollypops to Cigarettes*). Shashi flashbacked us to the story when we visited a dance bar in Mulund and got rounded up by the cops. We laughed together in the memories of that incident.

'Are the dance bars still there?' I asked.

'They are illegal now, but they still operate under the pretext of orchestra bars and not dance bars?' said Shashi.

'And what's the difference?' I asked

'Technically it means that girls can only shake a leg under the influence of a live band, but practically there is no difference,' smiled Shashi.

'Should we try an orchestra bar now?' Chirag threw the million-dollar question.

We looked at one another but said nothing. Our eyes said it all. It was a strong YES in the three pairs of eyes. And that was it. Within the next 45 minutes, we found ourselves in the 'Meenal Live Orchestra Bar' in Mulund. Twenty- five years later we were pseudo bachelors again. We danced to the live music while showering fifty and hundred rupees bills over the dancing dolls around us. We were there till the wee hours of the morning. And as I hailed a cab and travelled back to my service apartment in Chembur, I could only feel lucky to have taken the decision to pursue my career in Mumbai, away from Shreya in Gurgaon.

Within five minutes Manjari was fully aroused. By this time my hands had successfully got rid of her jeans. She ripped open my Tee and I gave the same treatment to her panties. I hugged her nude body tightly against mine, caressing her all over. Then I plunged her on the bed of my service apartment and dived on her.

I met Manjari at a conference held in Ramada Hotel Powai in April this year. I vaguely remember the conference was about Artificial Intelligence and Machine learning, AIML in short. This is a newly coined term in the corporate world and both Manjari and I were attending this conference to know more about AIML. During the first tea break, we literally bumped into each other rather by chance. Manjari was at the coffee counter trying to figure out how to dish out a coffee from the over-complicated machine. I was waiting just behind her with a cup in my hand, next in line to get a coffee. Finally, Manjari figured out the button that dished out the café latte. She gleefully filled her cup and turned around without realizing that I was waiting just behind her.

'Oops, I am so sorry,' said Manjari. She bumped into me, spilling a little bit of hot coffee on my shirt.

'I did not notice you at all,' she said, while I tried to wipe off the coffee with a tissue.

'It's OK, madam, I am not a personality to be noticed anyway,' I said with a smile.

She seemed a bit embarrassed by my witty comment.

'Are you here to attend the conference on AIML?' she asked, to tide over the embarrassment.

'Not exactly, I was just passing by and wanted to check if this coffee machine was working,' I said in a serious tone.

She took a few seconds to understand the joke, and then laughed out heartily. Though I am probably a bit too aged to appreciate laughter coming from a stranger lady, I could not help getting mesmerised at Manjari's ringing laughter. I laughed back too. We struck a conversation thereafter. The rest of the day we sat side by side in the conference hall. My interests from AIML had vanished by now and I focused more on Manjari. She had a perfect figure so to say. She was about 5 feet 4 inches with a perfect balance of chest and waist. She had sharp features, with an even sharper nose, deep brown eyes, and a perfect smile. She was dressed in a black salwar suit, with a perfect neckline plunge, revealing only the top of her cleavage. Please don't get me wrong after reading Manjari's description. I am no womanizer at all. In fact, after my marriage with Shreya, I had hardly met any female other than in my official capacity. But that day, something in Manjari rang a bell in me. Probably after twenty years, I felt young again. I wanted to know more about her and made the most of the conference to do so.

Manjari lived in Goregaon and she ran a proprietary marketing firm. She was an experienced marketer and a divorcee single mother of an eight-year-old son. The last part to me was more interesting than the first. Who knows, probably I too shall be a single divorcee soon. So, it was always good to build backups. By the end of the conference, Manjari and I had started to know each other better. I shared with her my job credentials and added the information that I lived alone in Mumbai. We had exchanged numbers and wanted to build a professional network. At the end of the day, I offered to buy her a quick drink before we left the hotel. Even as I asked her, I was reasonably sure that she would be politely declining the invitation. On the contrary, I was surprised when she accepted the offer without hesitance. So, we sat in the Ramada hotel bar on the ground floor and ordered our drinks.

'What would you have Manjari?' I asked.

'What are you having?' she asked me in return.

'I guess I shall settle for a black label, large,' I said.

'I shall go for the same.'

'Well, so are you a whisky lover too?' I asked.

'I try different tastes when it comes to alcohol, from whiskey to wine, everything.'

'You have the perfect company then, but beer is my favourite,' I smiled.

'Why not go for beers then?' she asked.

'Are you sure?' I double-checked.

'Absolutely.'

'Beers it is then, Heineken will do?' I asked.

'Sure, Heineken it is.'

We went on for five to six bottles each. I hardly had so much beer with a stranger, and that too a lady, before. Our conversation went around from alcohol to our education, work, hobbies, and our current state of life. I learned that her husband was a doctor and stayed in Gurgaon. They were divorced for two years now and Manjari and her son Pritam stayed in Mumbai. I guess we both enjoyed the evening. We parted with a tight hug and a promise to meet again.

The promise was kept, again and again. I was the first one to text her inviting her over dinner, about a week from our first meeting in Ramada. She promptly relented.

'You like fish?' I texted Manjari.

'Can I say no to fish when a Bong is inviting me for dinner?' she texted back.

So, we met at Mahesh Lunch Home, Juhu for dinner next Saturday. The dinner was followed by a walk on the Juhu beach. We relentlessly talked through the evening. It was almost midnight when I dropped her at her residence in Goregaon. Our next meeting was in Jazz by the Bay on the Marine drive. We went for diner after watching a film in the famous Eros theatre in South Mumbai. Post our dinner, we walked along the serene marine drive, this time hand in hand with our bodies suggestively close to each other.

Infidelity, is it? The question haunted me. Was my friendship with Manjari infidelity? Were we getting too close? Then what do I call the 'friendship' between Shreya and Dipankar, her ex-heartthrob in college? I know she and Dipankar still exchange texts and speak to each other often. No, I don't sneak-peek into Shreya's phone. She has openly said that to me.

Sometimes they have even met for dinner when she travels to Bangalore, where Dipankar runs his start-up venture. Once, he was traveling to Gurgaon and took Shreya out for dinner. When she came back it was 1 AM in the morning. I had lost it that day and Shreya and I had a ferocious fight over the matter. Was her relationship with Dipankar not infidelity? So, why couldn't I freely mix with Manjari? I tried to justify my holding hands with her on the Marine drive. But I kept the Manjari episode a secret from Shreya. That was making me feel guilty. To date, I did not keep any chapter of my life hidden from Shreya. But was she doing the same? Did she tell me all about Dipankar and her relationship? I justified once again my keeping Manjari a secret from Shreya.

Mumbai was giving me mixed feelings. On one hand, I was enjoying the company of old friends and my newly found friend. On the other, I missed my family, more so Abhijeet than Shreya. I also felt nostalgic when I passed through old memories of our life in Mumbai. One Sunday, I travelled to Borivali to see our house in Mumbai. The trip brought me back the romantic memories with Shreya. I still remember the days when we met every day after our office at the Borivali station, shared a single banana milkshake with two straws, and walked back hand in hand to our abode. I did not realise when that romance fled from our married life, so much so that I am holding a different set of hands, on the Marine Drive now. Once on an official field visit, I passed across the Jaslok Hospital where Abhijeet was born. I distinctly remember the anxious moments we spent in this hospital to see our only child. Though it was an expensive proposition, yet I could not keep myself from flying back to Gurgaon every now and then to see Abhijeet and to some extent Shreya too.

Manjari sat up on the bed and took charge of my jeans now. She stripped me off my belt first, followed by my jeans and finally my jocks. She pushed me on the bed and rolled her tongue suggestively all over my body. She then planted her lips and tongue just where I wanted them to be the most. I rolled my hands over her bare back as she laid on me. Our fondling lasted for the next forty minutes and then I went deep inside her. I don't remember having such fulfilling sex for a long time. It was only my fourth meeting with Manjari, this time in my service apartment. Manjari and I lay nude on my bed, both of us looked relentlessly satisfied with the proceedings of the evening. This was one secret that I would have to guard well from Shreya, I thought as Manjari and I started dressing up.

Chapter 14

THE YEAR OF THE PANDEMIC

(May 2021)

'This is what I call divine happiness,' I said to myself, as I lay in the Jacuzzi of our master bathroom with a beer can in my right hand. Water from eight jets in the Jacuzzi kept on giving me an ultimate aqua massage. This has been my typical Sunday routine for the last seven years since we shifted to Gurgaon. I lay in the Jacuzzi in the attached bath of our grand bedroom for almost an hour. While I took the aqua massage, I also gulped down two cans of beer. The beer brands keep changing every Sunday. While I do have the good old Kingfisher sometimes, but on most Sundays, I experiment with beers from across the globe – Corona from Mexico, Hoegaarden from Belgium, Singha from Singapore, and Suntory from Japan. I have them all in the wall-to-wall bar in my living room, probably my most prized possession. Post my bath I have a fixed lunch menu every Sunday – a quarter of a kilo of mutton along with plain rice. This has been my menu for the last two hundred Sundays at a stretch. After lunch too, I have a fixed Sunday agenda on my cards. Two hours of blissful Sunday afternoon siesta, with heavy curtains blocking the sunlight from our large master bedroom windows.

This is how I define divine happiness. Why do I call it so? Well, I had read thousands of definitions of happiness. But my Sunday agenda is my original way of defining the term. It signifies three things. First, I am rich enough to have a personal Jacuzzi in my master washroom. Second, I am healthy enough to be digesting a litre of imported beer and a quarter kilogram of mutton curry over the last two hundred Sundays, and that is without any cholesterol issues on my blood report. Last, but not least, I have a peaceful mind enough that allows me to nap for two hours on a Sunday afternoon.

Technically, you can call me quite a successful man as I cross through my forty-fifth year of life. A Director with PepsiCo married to a Director of Unilever. Handsome salaries are drawn from both ends. The family is complete with a ten-year-old son who attends the most expensive school in Gurgaon. A respectable bank account coupled with strong mutual fund investments. Owner of three residential properties in three large metro cities of the country. Currently living in a penthouse owned in Gurgaon. We bought the penthouse that we had rented earlier when we came to Gurgaon. Shreya's Merc E class and my Audi A6 class gracing the garage. Last year I finally dumped my old Toyota and graduated to an Audi as my career progressed further with PepsiCo

India. Last, but the best of wealth is my health which allows me to do at least three marathon runs every year.

As I lay in bliss in the Jacuzzi, my memories went back to the small bathroom decorated with white tiles in our Borivali condo just after our marriage. Almost on all Sundays, Shreya and I used to shower together in that small bathroom, the most romantic moments of the week it used to be. I don't remember having a bath with Shreya in this expensive Jacuzzi since we moved to Gurgaon. Was my lying alone in the tub with a beer the actual bliss or was it the beautiful memories in that small white bathroom the real happiness? I wondered as I sipped on my beer as jet-speed water continued to massage my naked body.

Things had not been going great with our relationship even after the COVID pandemic forced us both to stay at home continuously since March 2020. It had been more than a year now that both Shreya and I had been working from home due to the pandemic. I came back from Mumbai just before the lockdown last year and since then have been working remotely from Gurgaon. I was doing well as the GM sales in Mumbai, but suddenly the then Director Supply chain resigned from the company. I applied for this position through the internal job portal and bagged it easily owing to my previous supply chain experience. I was profusely happy with the move and the promotion. Firstly, I could come back to Gurgaon and be with my son, secondly, at least now Shreya won't be taunting me for being a senior manager or GM, I, at last, equated her in position and remuneration. I guess now I could meet the aspirations that Shreya had for her hubby. I also changed my dressing sense apart from my car. I bought a lot of expensive brands online but hardly got the chance to wear them since I had been working from home. Probably most of Shreya's complaints would have been taken care of. But things quiet did not go the way I thought.

Shreya and I continued to argue on something or the other. COVID 19 had forced us to spend more time together in the last year than we did in the last eighteen years of marriage. When I moved to Mumbai for the sales stint, I strongly hoped that a bit of absence from each other would bring back the flare in our relationship. It did not work. Then I moved back to Gurgaon in March last year and immediately COVID 19 forced us to stay together. I hoped that spending all twenty-four hours together, stuck in a room would bring us back close again. Instead, with all our time, our distance increased. Mental health was a new term coined during the lockdown. Probably that's what was amiss with both of us. With the 'work from home', both our working hours as well as stress level shot up. We did not even realise that our eight to nine-hour workdays were being extended to twelve to thirteen hours. And managing a business and team remotely needed skill sets that the normal office-going corporates lacked. To add to this stress, was the depression of Abhijeet. The poor ten-year-old had nowhere to vent out his energy. No school, no friends, no tennis class, no soccer games. He did not know how to spend time. We tried to glue him to all kinds of online sessions – coding, singing, drama, et al. But it did not work. We hardly at any time left in a day to spend with Abhijeet. To be honest, we spent more time with him when life was normal. When I worked in Gurgaon, before the pandemic, I used to come home from the office and spend time with my son, sometimes playing indoor games, sometimes watching a movie, or reading a book. In the last year, both Shreya and I had little bandwidth to spend time with Abhijeet. We didn't realise that our energetic son was slowly sinking into depression.

Across the globe, the pandemic had probably caused more mental damage than physical harm. The death rates were low, but the mental health of people was in danger. Many lost their earnings. Shreya and I had our mailboxes flooded with CVs looking for a job. While people like us who were still earning did not know where to spend. All recreational avenues were absent. No cinema, no shopping malls, no pubs, no restaurants, and no vacations. In the corporate world, people forgot to take leaves. But now there was nowhere to go after taking a leave, so why take any? Suddenly we realised that we need so little as essentials in life. All our spending was for non-essential substances. Only buying weekly groceries was so cheap. All these years we had been spending fortunes trying to recreate ourselves. The fancy cars, designer clothes, expensive five-star dinners, and international vacations were of no use in this pandemic year. For many corporate professionals like us, days and weeks, and months were being spent just working, eating, and sleeping. Day after day this routine was silently impacting our well-being. This had started impacting our son too. Finally, in December last year, we decided to take a road trip even at the cost of exposing ourselves to the novel coronavirus.

Shreya, Abhijeet, and I drove her Merc all the way up to Shimla from Gurgaon. We planned to spend our last week of December 2020 in the lap of nature. It was our first vacation after almost fifteen months. We did not wish to risk flying through airports, hence had to choose a destination to which we could safely drive, with only one break. Hence, we chose Shimla.

'We can start very early in the morning. We can pack a few sandwiches for breakfast,' I said.

'What do we do for lunch?' asked Shreya.

'We can drive for straight five to six hours and reach Chandigarh by lunchtime,' I replied.

'Will it be safe to have lunch on a highway?' she inquired.

'Not on the highway, we shall drive into Chandigarh city and have lunch at the Taj. That should be safe,' I said.

Shreya agreed at once. So, we finally executed the vacation plan on 24th December 2020. We drove to Chandigarh, had a lunch break at the Taj, and then drove uphill to Shimla. We all felt much relaxed in the next few days in the lap of nature. We could feel our mind and body responding to the change of climate and topography. We had been literally locked in our penthouse for many months and this was a welcome change. I was grateful to Shreya for making this plan. On new year's eve, the three of us sat on our suite balcony gazing at the stars while sipping single malt. Abhijeet, of course, was sipping hot chocolate. Sitting by the fire in near-zero temperature, surrounded by the Himalayas, with a single malt glass in hand was a divine experience no doubt. I silently wished that we all have a better 2021. May our relationship find a stronger foothold. May Abhijeet become an energetic and happy child once again. May the pandemic go away. May the year give enough vaccines to India and may we all get vaccinated. May we prosper safely and be together once again. Little did I know, just like our country's government, that the pandemic was far from over in the dawning of January 2021.

Knock…Knock… Someone knocked on the bathroom door

'Are you done, with your bath?' shouted Shreya from outside the door.

'Why?' I asked, 'can't I have a peaceful Sunday bath?'

'Take as much time as you want, I am skipping lunch and going for a nap?' said Shreya from outside the door.

'That's strange, on weekdays our meetings clash and we cannot have lunch together. At least let us have the Sunday lunch together Shreya.' I said, gulping down the balance of the beer.

'I am not feeling well, have a slight fever. You and Abhijeet carry on,' she said.

At once I walked out of the Jacuzzi. This pandemic was a time when a slight fever can run down a trickle of fear down the spine. I wiped myself and wore a robe and came out of the bathroom at once. By the time, Shreya was already in bed wrapped in a blanket.

'What's wrong, let me check,' I asked moving closer to the bed.

'Nothing, just a bit of fever and body ache,' she said.

'That's pretty frightful. These are likely COVID symptoms,' I said anxiously.

'No. It just might me petty fever from the changing weather,' Shreya said reassuringly.

But I was not reassured at all. The thought of COVID in my house ran me cold.

'Shall I arrange for a COVID test, Shreya?' I asked.

'You are worrying too much. I should be fine by the evening. Please go for lunch and let me sleep.'

I came out of the room to the dining hall. Abhijeet and I quietly had lunch. The mutton seemed to have no taste at all. After a long time, I was deeply worried about Shreya's health.

After lunch, I tried to have my siesta in Abhijeet's room.

'Why are you in my room? I want to watch a movie now. Go to your room.' Abhijeet complained.

'I can't go to the master bedroom, Mamma is sleeping there,' I said.

'Go and sleep beside her no dad, leave my room,' said my son.

'Your mom has symptoms of COVID, we cannot go near her now, till she gets checked,' I explained.

Not sure, how much he understood, but he did not object to my sleeping on his bed any further. He slowly walked out of the room, probably to have a sneak peek into his mom's room. 'What a disease,' I wondered. It does not let a son into his mom's room and prevents a husband to sleep with his wife. No matter how much I tried, I could not have my siesta today. Worries kept cropping into my mind. I tried to chide off the worry by convincing myself that Shreya just had viral flu and nothing else. But the negative thought kept crawling back again and again. It is probably true that the more one thinks negatively about an event, the more likely the event would turn out to be negative. By evening, Shreya was burning with fever. She could hardly speak. I checked her with the thermometer, 102 degrees Fahrenheit said the scale. Worry surely crept into me. She did not eat anything for dinner. I was truly worried. I made some saline water and tried to make her drink it. She could not take it in. She brought it out immediately. Though I had been advising Abhijeet to stay away from his mom, I could not practise what I preached. I lay beside Shreya the whole night, checking her temperature and oxygen levels from time to time.

The next morning, I called Dr Maan, our family physician. She advised me to get Shreya's swab test for COVID done immediately. After three hours of frantic search on the net for testing labs, I could finally convince one lab to come home and collect the swab sample. They agreed to do so at a whopping price and promised to get back with the test results in 48 hours. The next two days were spent in sheer agony as we waited for the test results to come by. Shreya, in the meantime, showed little sign of improvement. Her fever dipped slightly with a heavy dose of paracetamol and then shot back again once the effect of the dose was over. She had hardly eaten any solid food over the last two days. Everything she tried to take in, came out immediately. All she could have was some glucose water and saline water. I did not log in to the office for the last 48 hours. Worry had crippled me all over.

Finally, after two days our worst fear was confirmed. Shreya was COVID positive. The second wave of COVID had hit her below the belt.

———

Chapter 15

Till Death Do Us Part

(June 2021)

Once again, I found myself outside the ICU, while Shreya lay inside. The same chain of the hospital too. In 2008 it was Fortis, Kandivali Mumbai, and exactly thirteen years later it was Fortis Gurgaon. The only difference being that this time I was not allowed to go inside the ICU as it was a special COVID ward.

Within five days of testing COVID positive, Shreya's condition had started deteriorating. She had constant fever along with body ache and nausea. Coupled with that she had developed incessant coughing. Our doctor had advised checking her oxygen levels and fever at least five times daily. For the first four days, though her fever hovered between 101 to 102 degrees, her oxygen levels remained steady at 97. It was from the fifth day that her oxygen level started dropping below 90. I frantically reached out to the doctor. She advised me to take her for a few blood tests and a chest CT scan. So, I did. The results came a day later, and they were not encouraging at all. My panic began to rise. By the sixth day,

Shreya's oxygen level dropped to 80. As per our physician, Shreya's condition was critical and she needed to be oxygenated immediately, either at home or at a hospital. The doctor's verdict seemed very simple, but what transpired in trying to get Shreya into a hospital was much more ferocious than a nightmare.

I was very reluctant to send Shreya to a hospital. So, as a first step, I tried to organise an oxygen cylinder at home. The question that came to my mind was where do we find an oxygen cylinder? As most of us would do, I tried googling it. As I started googling, fear set in. All sorts of news flashes started appearing on my phone. I was completely oblivious of the situation around the country due to the pandemic. It seemed from the newsflashes on the internet that oxygen cylinders and concentrators were the most demanded product in the nation at that time, more so it was next to impossible to get one. I was lost. In most situations of distress, my usual reaction was always to get hassled and confused on the next steps. Shreya's reaction was always the opposite, she stayed calm in distress and could think of solutions. How I missed her now! But I could not possibly share the news about the oxygen distress with her when the SPo2 of her blood was below 80. What do I do now? I was almost in tears. I tried WhatsApp as my next mode of oxygen hunting. I dropped a message in all the groups I was a member of, school group, college group, society group, and all the office groups. I did get replies for sure. Most were messages of 'get well soon', 'we shall pray for her' types and completely useless in the situation that I was in. But there was a silver lining, I did get some leads about oxygen suppliers in Gurgaon. I left no stones unturned. I called every number that came as a lead. But in vain, most numbers were either switched off or not reachable. The ones I could reach over to did not have any oxygen cylinders available. At last, as a ray of hope, one person replied that they did have one cylinder left. At that point, I felt that I have got the moon in my hand.

'Sir, we do have one filled cylinder, but it will cost fifty thousand rupees,' said the voice on the other end of my cell phone.

'Absolutely no problem, please send me the cylinder and I shall pay immediately,' I said. At that point, I could have paid anything to save Shreya.

'Sir, we take payment in advance, you have to transfer the money via google pay, and the cylinder along with tube and mask shall reach your home in less than an hour,' said the voice.

Without hesitation, I wired fifty grants to the unknown owner of the voice. Within two minutes I got a call back from the man.

'We received the money, sir, please text your address and the cylinder will reach you shortly.'

'I will do that immediately, please send the cylinder, my wife's oxygen level is at 78,' I replied frantically.

'Don't worry at all, sir, we shall all pray for her,' said the voice and disconnected the call.

I sighed in relief. Now within the next hour, Shreya would be oxygenated. Thanks to the unknown voice that came as help from Sai baba, I thought. I went and sat beside Shreya in the bedroom. She was coughing uncontrollably and gasped for breath. I caressed her over. A tear trickled down my cheek. I had never seen her in such a dire state before. There were full chances that I may also get infected by the deadly virus. But I did not care. I kept Abhijeet safe, locked in another bedroom along with Aarti, our maid. I wish I could take away Shreya's pain. I wished that the virus left her alone and infected me. In the last two years, Shreya and I were struggling to keep our relationship going, and in the last two hours, I felt so strongly for her that I was ready to do anything for her.

'Shreya, bear the pain for an hour, oxygen is not its way,' I smiled and tried to cheer her up.

She kept quiet, not on purpose, but she was unable to speak as she gasped for breath. I kept on looking at my watch. Forty minutes had passed since I had the last dialogue with the oxygen man. I hope it soon arrives. Another forty minutes went by, but the cylinder was yet to come. I was becoming more and more anxious. I re-dialled the number. It was switched off. Shit. Every five minutes I kept on trying the number again, but it was still switched off. It took me another 5 calls to realise that I had been duped. No oxygen cylinder was going to arrive. I sobbed uncontrollably. Shreya's oxygen level had dropped to 69. What do I do now? I called doctor Maan once again.

'Hospitalise her immediately,' came her short reply.

'Do you know of any hospital where I can find a bed for her?' I asked.

The call was disconnected, probably even the doctor did not know of any vacant beds in this dire pandemic.

The next few hours that I spend that night were probably the most dreadful five hours of my life. Even more dreadful than the 26th July 2005 night I spend sitting on top of an SUV in the Mumbai floods. That night it was my life at stake, and this time it was Shreya's. I realised that my life would be meaningless without hers. By this time Shreya's oxygen level was gradually moving southwards. She was already at 65. For the first time, I did not get confused about what I should do next. I once again messaged for help, 'Desperately seeking for a hospital bed for Shreya' in all sorts of social media that I was a part of. But this time I did not wait for a response. Only action can reduce anxiety. I picked up Shreya and carried her into the basement garage. She could hardly walk and incessantly gasped for air. I put her in the back seat of my car and darted off to the nearest hospital. Come what may, even if I need to empty my life savings, I shall get her a bed before dawn, I pledged. For the next five hours, I drove from one hospital to the other. First to Paras Hospital, then to Pratiksha, Max, Apollo, I left no stone unturned. But the result was in vain. None of them had ICU beds available. What I experienced that night, I would like to forget, but possibly won't be able to. While my Shreya was gasping for her breath in the back seat of an Audi, there were so many more wives, daughters, sons, fathers, mothers, and even children who were pleading for ICU beds and oxygen. For a moment I felt that Shreya's last bed would be the back seat of an Audi A6. What a bed for a brand-conscious corporate director! I was unable to take the stress anymore, I parked by the road and wept with my head drooping on the steering wheel. I was probably at the end of the road of hope. I would probably not be able to drive Shreya back home.

The miraculous call came on my phone exactly at 5.10 AM. While the first streak of the sun was showing up in the dawning sky, probably my hopes to save Shreya got some light.

'Listen, there's no point asking how you are, as your FB post speaks of your distress,' said the female voice.

'Manjari. How on earth? How are you?' I did not know how to react to Manjari's call when Shreya was dying in the back seat of my car.

'Did you get a bed for Shreya or do you still need help? How is she now?' asked Manjari.

In the last twelve months since the pandemic, I had very little contact with Manjari. Obviously, I did not meet her as I never went to Mumbai during this period. Apart from a few formal greeting exchanges over WhatsApp, there had been no major conversations with her. Neither she nor I called each other in the twelve months. And, in the direst of my state, she calls me in the wee hours of the morning, enquiring about Shreya's health.

'Not yet, Manjari. I don't think I will be able to save her. I lost, Manjari. I could not give anything to Shreya. I could not keep her happy when she was living with me and I could not give her medical care in her dying moments.' I suddenly broke down into loud sobs. All through the night, I could not vent out my agony, lest Shreya gets disturbed. Now with Manjari calling me, I could not check myself anymore.

'Calm down, Abhi. I called to help you. I have organised a bed for her,' said Manjari.

I could not believe my ears. Was what I heard true?

'My ex-husband, Pallav, is the Head of administration with Fortis Gurgaon. I called him and told him about your state. He is ready to help. I am texting you his number, speak to him and an ICU bed will be arranged,' Manjari said in one breath.

The rest of the game was as easy as a cakewalk. I called Pallav, Manjari' s ex. I did not know him, yet he did all the needful for me. By 7 AM the morning, Shreya was admitted to the ICU of Fortis Gurgaon. By then, her oxygen level was well below 50. Her CT scan was done, and it showed more than 80% lung infection. As per the doctors, her condition was supercritical.

As I sat on the bench outside the ICU, several thoughts passed my mind, some about Shreya and me and some about the dire affairs in the country today. How much had I troubled Shreya? I could not keep her happy through the eighteen years of our relationship. She did not want much from me. She was not like the nagging Indian housewife. Probably I did not know how to manage a successful wife. What did she want? Just a bit of ambition in my career. Why could not I give her that? Probably I could have fast-tracked my career to keep her happy? She wanted me to dress well. Couldn't I have done that, just for her happiness? She wanted me to drive a good car, was it for her benefit. I could have well afforded the Audi long ago, why didn't I do it? How much I have insulted her for helping his friend Dipankar, it was her money and she had every right to do so. Why did I not let her? She wanted me to spend more constructive time with Abhijeet. Shouldn't I have done that as a father for my only child? Why did I cheat on her? Why did I sleep with Manjari? Please give me one more chance Sai baba, I thought as tears kept on moistening my face. I promise I shall keep

Shreya delighted for the rest of my days. Please, all I wanted is one more chance.

My tried body gradually leaned against the ICU visitor's bench. I had no knowledge of how Shreya was inside. Finally, I could not take the anxiety anymore, I lay flat on the bench. I could not help to spare a prayer for the state that India was in today. How fortunate I was to get my wife a bed with Manjari's divine help. There were so many wives, husbands, and sons dying on the street in the pandemic. And our government just looked on as the disaster struck on the country's face. Common people were gasping for oxygen and there was none. The country's health care system was gasping for breath itself, how could it have prevented numerous deaths. No politicians or capitalists were to be seen anywhere. They were busy trying to hide from the virus themselves. The government sources were working a double shift to collate actual data on the deaths in the country, while death was playing havoc every day. I could not think anymore. I could feel that fatigue and sleep were overpowering me. The owner of three villas and luxury cars and handsome bank accounts finally fell asleep on a steel bench outside the ICU of a hospital as his wife was battling with death inside the closed door. Health is indeed the most precious wealth. The pandemic had reasserted that naked truth to all Indians. All I prayed for was a second chance. I love you Shreya, I love you too much to lose you… Teardrops fell on the ground as I passed into a deep sleep.

'Mr. Bhattacharya, hello… Mr. Bhattacharya… sir… hello…Mr. Bhattacharya…'

I woke up suddenly and sprang up on the bench. Two doctors in their full COVID safety gear were standing in front of me, trying to wake me up.

'Are you all right, Sir,' asked one of the blue-robed doctors.

'Yes, what happened? How is my wife?' I asked anxiously.

'Would you mind stepping aside with us please, we need to talk urgently,' said the second doctor as they both walked away from the bench towards the ICU door.

What happened to Shreya, I thought, as I swiftly got on my feet and started following the doctors. I could hear my heart pounding loudly as Shreyas serene face glimpsed across my mind. I hope… I just hope… I see that face smiling again.

———

ANECDOTE

(July 2022)

'Abhijeet, don't take off your jacket, you will catch a cold,' Manjari yelled at Abhijeet, just like a mother.

Abhijeet and Pritam, Manjari's son, were playing on the hotel lawn, while Manjari was babysitting them.

Shreya and I sat on a bench at the edge of the cliff, holding hands, and our bodies tightly close together. We were mesmerised to see the sun gradually setting on the Swiss Alps, changing the colour of the mountains.

I could not see Pallav around. Probably he had hidden somewhere to have a puff on his cigarette. Poor Pallav. He had to hide while smoking, lest Manjari chewed his brain off for touching the butt.

Shreya, Abhijeet, and I along with Manjari, Pallav, and their son Pritam came on a vacation to Murren, Switzerland. Murren is a beautiful virgin Swiss village hidden high in the Swiss Alps. My pen does not have power enough to describe the beauty of

Murren. It seemed like we were sitting in midst of a picture postcard and Murren's beauty could not be real. For both the families, this was a vacation after two and a half years. At last, the Covid pandemic was done and dusted with and the world came back to normalcy.

Yes, after eighteen days of battling with COVID, last June, finally Shreya emerged as the winner. Luckily the virus did not dare to touch me, even after I spent eighteen nights sitting on a bench just outside the COVID ward. Shreya is a sure shot fighter, even the docs in Fortis Hospital acknowledged that. They had almost lost hope, but my prayers did not. Finally, Shreya's will overpowered the disease. The day I brought her home from Fortis Hospital, I filled my car's back seat with chocolates and candies, just like I had done when I brought her to our Borivali flat the first time we landed in Mumbai. I really felt our marriage got a second chance.

What those eighteen days of disease did to Shreyas and my relationship, our eighteen years of marriage could not. All our differences were wiped off. Shreya and I once again realised that we could not do without each other. We did not care what our bank balance was or what our corporate designations were. I did not care with whom Shreya was meeting and she did not care about what I was wearing. All we cared about was each other and our son Abhijeet. After a brief turmoil of eighteen nights, COVID gave our relation new sunshine for years to come.

Not only did COVID bring us together as a family, but it also reunited another divorced family. While checking on Shreya's health during those eighteen days, Manjari had once again started conversing with her ex-husband Pallav. Probably cupid shot his arrow once again and just as Shreya recovered, Manjari shared the news with me about her reuniting with Pallav. Shortly after, Manjari and Pritam moved from Mumbai to Gurgaon and started living with Pallav. At least, the pandemic rekindled a few lives though it took away many.

Manjari started her own consulting business in Gurgaon while Dr Pallav still saved lives as the Head of administration of Fortis Hospital. After Shreya recovered fully, one evening we went to Manjari's house with flowers and wine to profusely thank her and Pallav. We fully acknowledge that without their intervention, Shreya could not be saved on that dreadful night. Since our meeting that evening, gradually Manjari and Pallav became our family friends. Of course, Manjari and I secretly pledged to keep that evening in my Mumbai apartment as a secret from our families ever after. History cannot be undone, but Manjari and I promised that history would not repeat itself for sure.

'Time for some rum and coke, guys,' I heard Pallav's voice.

Shreya and I got up from the bench we were sitting on and walked up to Manjari and Pallav. They had already set table and chairs in the middle of the lawn. There was Coke and Captain Morgan rum on the table along with fried pork ribs.

'The evening is all set it seems,' I said as I settled on a chair.

Within the next 15 minutes, all six of us were settled around the table as Pallav poured rum and coke for the adults and just coke for Abhijeet and Pritam.

As our glasses clinked in the July evening amidst the Swiss Alps, the beauty of the mountains was as if wishing us a very beautiful married life ahead.

Cheers!